Twister

www.**rbooks**.co.uk

Twister

A CODE RED ADVENTURE

CHRIS RYAN

DOUBLEDAY

TWISTER
A DOUBLEDAY BOOK 978 0 385 61297 5
TRADE PAPERBACK 978 0 385 61298 2

Published in Great Britain by Doubleday,
an imprint of Random House Children's Books
A Random House Group Company

This edition published 2008

1 3 5 7 9 10 8 6 4 2

Copyright © Chris Ryan, 2008

The Random House Group Limited supports the Forest Stewardship Council
(FSC), the leading international forest certification organization. All our titles
that are printed on Greenpeace-approved FSC-certified paper carry the FSC logo.
Our paper procurement policy can be found at www.rbooks.co.uk/environment.

Mixed Sources
Product group from well-managed
forests and other controlled sources
FSC   www.fsc.org Cert no. TT-COC-2139
© 1996 Forest Stewardship Council

Set in 13.5/l7.5pt Garamond by Falcon Oast Graphic Art Ltd.

RANDOM HOUSE CHILDREN'S BOOKS
61–63 Uxbridge Road, London W5 5SA

www.kidsatrandomhouse.co.uk
www.rbooks.co.uk

Addresses for companies within The Random House Group Limited can be
found at: www.randomhouse.co.uk/offices.htm

THE RANDOM HOUSE GROUP Limited Reg. No. 954009

A CIP catalogue record for this book is available from the British Library.

Printed and bound in Great Britain by Clays Ltd, St Ives plc

A CODE RED ADVENTURE

Location:
Florida, USA

Prologue

A small island in the Indian Ocean. Around midnight.

The little girl's name was Basheera. In the island language it meant Bringer of Joy. But there was no joy in that small house tonight. Only sadness.

Basheera lay on her bed, her frail body lit up by the dim electric light that hung from the ceiling. Her breathing was heavy and noisy, and her parents knew just what that meant. They sat on either side of her, each of them holding one of their daughter's hands. Neither of them said a word. There was nothing to do but wait.

A blanket covered the lower part of Basheera's body. It was not there to keep her warm – it was a hot, humid night anyway – but because the adults could not bear to look at her legs. Those legs that they had watched grow strong since she was a baby, now bloodied and broken because of the men and their machines.

She opened her eyes. Basheera's mother gasped. A miracle! But it soon became clear that although her eyes were open, they saw nothing, and they flickered shut again. Her mother put her free hand against the girl's forehead. It burned. The two adults cast worried glances at each other before returning to their silent vigil.

When the men had come, with their diggers and their machines, everyone had known it meant trouble. Before long the bulldozers had moved in, clearing trees from the forest that was so precious to these villagers, and preparing to dig for the thing they spoke of as if it were the most precious substance on earth: oil.

The children, of course, had been transfixed by the big machines, just as the grown-ups had been suspicious of them. Despite warnings from their parents and shouts from the men, they had played games around them. It had really been only a matter of time before an accident happened. It had just been a question of to whom.

If it had been someone other than Basheera who had been caught under the heavy wheels of the bulldozer, her parents would have been sorrowful too. Theirs was a true community: they shared each other's happiness and they felt each other's pain. But when they had seen their daughter's body, damaged beyond repair, their anguish had overcome them. It could not have been put into words.

The men responsible had washed their hands of it. It was Basheera's own fault, they said. She should not have been where she was. But all the villagers had known this was not true. Basheera had had every right to be there. It was the newcomers who had been trespassing.

The villagers had rallied around. The chief had declared that all their resources should be directed towards saving the life of the little girl. They had tapped the deep-red sap of the dragon's blood tree – a well-known cure-all – to wash her damaged legs, but that had not been enough. They had performed sacred rituals, but still Basheera had grown more and more ill. There had been talk of taking her to a hospital on the mainland, but she could not have been moved.

And now it was clear that all anyone could do was pray for her soul, and curse the invaders who, in their greed, had caused this to happen.

Basheera's last breath was long. It sounded as if her soul was escaping from her body. In the silence that followed, her mother started shaking her head, as if refusing to believe that her daughter had passed away. But the signs were all too obvious: she was no longer breathing, and her chest had stopped moving up and down.

She had been dead for a full minute when her mother screamed. It was a pitiful sound, an inhuman shriek that echoed not just around their poor house, but around the whole village. Basheera's father gently let his daughter's hand fall, then hurried round to hug his wife, to give her some kind of comfort in that moment when there was no comfort to give.

Everyone in the village knew what the scream meant, of course, and before long they were gathering outside the house. There was a painful silence as Basheera's father emerged, carrying his daughter's lifeless body in his arms.

'This is what these people have done!' he roared in the language of the region. 'First they destroy our land, now they destroy our children! It must not continue!'

The villagers muttered their agreement as Basheera's father turned towards the chief of the village. 'It is your responsibility,' he intoned. 'You are our chief. You must see to it that these invaders leave our land. Basheera's brother, he has spent much time in the West. He will do what is necessary to avenge his sister. And there are others too. Others in the village who will help. You know who they are.'

The chief was a tall, gaunt man. His face was deeply lined and his eyes were dark. He nodded solemnly and the crowd grew silent to hear what he had to say in his deep, rich voice.

'These men think we are stupid. They think we are savages. They do not understand that we choose to live like we always have. They do not understand that we are like a sleeping snake – quiet when left alone, but deadly when angered. I swear to you now, over the body of this dead child, that this will not continue.' He turned to Basheera's mother and father. 'They will suffer as you have suffered. I do not care if it costs all our money or all our lives. They will leave our land and never come back. That is my promise to you, as long as I am your chief.'

His words resounded in the air, and they seemed to satisfy the assembled villagers, who voiced their approval before melting away into the night. Soon, only one of the crowd remained. He was a small man, but muscular. There was an angry scar along the left-hand side of his face and his eyes burned with a zealous fire. The chief looked at him seriously, pointed at him and then nodded. The scarred man nodded back and smiled. It was as though he had been chosen to do something, and that choice had made him glad.

Without saying a word, the two of them left, and then there was no one remaining outside the house. No one except Basheera's mother and father, helplessly clutching the cold, still body of their little girl, knowing that their life would never, ever be the same again.

Chapter One

Many thousands of miles away. Two weeks later.

It was the evenings that Ben Tracey liked most of all. The air would be full of the smell of wood smoke from the barbecue, and the red sun would be setting dreamily beyond the horizon, lighting up the flat sea with its warm glow.

It had been a good holiday and Ben felt he had deserved it. His holidays had a funny habit of going wrong, so there had been something rather blissful about two weeks by a beach in the Cayman Islands. His friends back at school had been jealous when they had heard he was going to be sunning himself on Grand Cayman courtesy of an old family friend who lived out there; they'd been doubly jealous when they'd heard he'd be flying out by himself, without any parents to cramp his style.

Ben couldn't help but smile at the thought of their faces when he had told them where he'd be staying. The house that Alec Ardler – an old teacher of his father's who always reminded Ben of pictures he'd seen of Albert Einstein – owned was ramshackle, but it was right on the beach. Open the gate at the bottom of the garden and you could walk straight out onto the fine golden sand. Beyond that was the sea, blue and clear like you normally only saw on postcards. It was the rainy season, which meant the beaches weren't as full as they might otherwise have been, but when the rain came it was in short, sharp bursts that cleared the air and made it all the more pleasant to be outside. The rest of the time, it was glorious sunshine.

Ben had known Alec for as long as he could remember. They'd always got on well, but he hadn't seen the old man for years, so he would have been excited to receive the invitation to spend his half term with him even if Alec hadn't retired to the Cayman Islands. He must have been comfortably in his eighties, but he was surprisingly spry for his age, and his mind was as agile as his body. He was one of those grown-ups who refused to talk down to anyone. Ben liked that. He liked the way Alec left him to his own devices; he liked the way that when they met for their regular dinner of barbecued fish in the garden, he sounded genuinely interested in what Ben had to say. He was a bit odd at times, a bit intense, but over the course of the two weeks, Ben felt that he had renewed a good friendship. So much so that he had opened up to him about the events of the previous couple of years – the floods in London, the fires in Adelaide, the horrible events of the Congo. He'd been a bit more reticent about what had happened at the military base in the UK, but in general he had told Alec more about his adventures than anyone else.

'Regular little harbinger of doom, aren't you, matey?' the old man had said. Ben just grimaced ruefully.

And now the holiday was nearly at an end. Just a couple more days and he would be flying back to England. Back to school and the dreary surroundings of his everyday life. He wasn't much looking forward to it and as he sat outside with Alec that evening, nursing a glass of chilled mango juice, he sighed heavily.

'Penny for your thoughts?' Alec asked quietly. He had a habit of using old-fashioned phrases like that.

Ben smiled. 'Oh, I don't know,' he said. 'Just thinking about going home.'

The dying embers of the wood crackled on the barbecue, and Alec nodded. 'Got a taste for the good life, eh? Don't blame you. Still, your parents will be looking forward to seeing you.'

'Yeah, I know, it's just—' Ben stopped talking and looked at Alec curiously. 'What's the matter?' he asked.

Alec's brow was furrowed. He was looking past Ben and out to sea. Ben followed his gaze and immediately saw what had grabbed his friend's attention. It was the sky. Minutes ago it had been like it always was at this time of the evening, flecked with pinks and oranges from the sun. But not now. Above them the sky was still clear, but now it was impossible to make out the horizon. In the distance the sea looked dark grey and seemed to merge into the sky, which was suddenly full of huge, bubbling clouds. It was as though they were being surrounded.

The two of them fell silent as they watched this peculiar weather formation. When Alec spoke, it was almost under his breath. 'I've been here a long time,' he said. 'I've never seen anything quite like that. Amazing thing, nature. Always got a surprise up its sleeve.'

'Looks to me like a storm is coming.'

Alec turned his head to look straight at Ben. There was something piercing in his eyes. 'Oh,' he said, 'a storm is coming all right. A storm is always coming. From everything you've told me, you should know that better than most. It's just a question of when.'

Ben blinked, unsure how to reply. It was such a strange thing to say. He had the feeling that Alec was talking about something other than the weather, but he didn't know what.

A chill descended and Ben shivered slightly. Alec stood up promptly. 'Come on,' he said. 'It's cold. If you're supposed to go diving with Angelo early tomorrow we should hit the hay.'

Ben nodded, relieved that the weird moment seemed to have passed. He stood up too and made his way indoors; though as he did so he couldn't help but notice that Alec lingered slightly, looking out to sea with an unknowable expression on his face. 'It won't last,' the old man said almost to himself. 'Be right as rain in the morning.'

Darkness fell, but the two men in the beaten-up old Ford parked fifty metres down the road had no plans to go home. They had sat there all day, all the night before and for several days and nights previously. They took it in turns to sleep and ate sparingly from their stash of food, only leaving the car to find somewhere to use for a toilet. They were both dark-skinned but one of them – the one who sat in the driver's seat – was a lot smaller than the other, and had a deep scar down the left-hand side of his face. It was his turn to keep watch now. He did so intently while his partner slept, keeping his gaze fixed on the ornate villa beyond.

They had already staked the place out, of course, when they first arrived. They knew that if anyone left for a period of time they would do so by car. And as this was the only road that led to the house, they could be sure of knowing when that happened.

Just so long as they kept watching. Kept vigilant. Kept their minds on the job in hand.

He looked at his watch. Eight p.m. Changeover time. He nudged his partner, whose eyes opened immediately. To look at him you'd think he had never been asleep.

'Your watch,' he said in a language that was never heard in this part of the world.

His partner nodded. 'Anything?' he asked.

The man shook his head. 'Nothing. Not yet. There will be, though. They can't stay in there for ever. Don't lose your concentration.'

With that the man closed his eyes and almost instantly fell asleep.

Ben slept fitfully. It wasn't the heat of the night or the mosquitoes that kept him awake. It was the constant visions of bubbling skies and black seas that seemed to drift through his dreams. He woke up the next morning feeling like he had hardly slept at all, but as he opened the shutters of his bedroom and looked out over the dawn sunrise, he was happy to see that the sky was as clear as it had ever been.

Alec had been right. The storm had passed, and Ben could enjoy the last two days of his holiday. And even though it was very early, he knew that Angelo would already be waiting for him.

Angelo Bandini was a lot more used to the luxuries of the Cayman Islands than Ben. He was a bit shorter than Ben, but a good deal more tanned, with long dark hair and deep brown eyes. He was one of those people you could tell was rich just by looking at him: expensive clothes, all the latest gadgets. His dad was a successful businessman – something to do with oil, Ben had worked out, though Angelo seldom talked about it – and had a house on Grand Cayman just next to Alec's, as well as several others dotted around the world. There were quite a few differences between Alec's simple place and Angelo's, however. For a start, Alec didn't have men with guns at the door. Angelo was holidaying without his parents, but he was very far from being alone. He didn't like calling the burly American guy who shadowed him everywhere he went a bodyguard, but that was what he was.

They had met on the first day of the holiday and Ben had innocently asked his new friend what the deal was with all the security. Angelo had blushed. 'It's just my dad,' he'd explained evasively in an English that put Ben's lack of Italian to shame – a result of the years of schooling Angelo had had in America. Ben sensed that it wouldn't be a good idea to press the matter. 'Hey' – his new friend had changed the subject – 'you know how to scuba dive?'

Ben had grinned. 'Not really,' he said. 'But there's a first time for everything, isn't there?'

Angelo had been a patient teacher. They'd started out in his father's swimming pool. It had only taken a couple of days for Ben to get the hang of it before his Italian friend had decided he was good enough to take the plunge into the sea. And once that had happened, Ben felt he was hooked for life. They had gone diving every day – sometimes twice a day – and Ben was keen to fit in as much as he could before it was time to leave.

He quickly threw on some clothes, tiptoed out of the house to avoid waking Alec, then hurried round to Angelo's house.

Angelo's guards were used to Ben by now and he was allowed into the beach-facing garden without any problems. His Italian friend was already waiting for him there, the scuba-diving gear at his feet and an expectant smile on his face. '*Sei pronto, Ben?*' he asked in his musical Italian accent. 'Are you ready?'

'Sure am,' Ben replied. He looked up to the sky. 'Hey, did you see the storm clouds last night?'

Angelo gave him a strange look. 'Storm clouds? No, Ben, I did not see any storm clouds. The sky is clear.'

Ben gave a moment's thought to explaining, but then decided not to. The sea was calling, and he could tell they were both eager to get started. Together they gathered up the equipment and trudged down to the beach where Angelo's speedboat – a sleek white machine – was moored, one of Angelo's father's helpers already aboard. There was no one else there at this early hour, just a few birds paddling on the wet sand and occasionally burrowing their beaks to look for food. Ben and Angelo waded out to the boat, carrying their gear above their heads, then slung it in and clambered aboard. As Angelo started up the motor himself, Ben noticed the ever-present figure of one of his bodyguards watching them from the shore.

The beach was shallow, so they had to motor a little way out to get enough depth for diving. By the time Angelo stopped the boat and let down the heavy motorized anchor, the bodyguard was just a dot in the distance. It was incredibly peaceful out here; their on-surface helper was so quiet he was almost invisible and there was nothing else but the splashing of the sea against the side of the boat for company. The two friends remained silent as they donned their canisters and masks before throwing themselves backwards over the side of the vessel.

The water was cold but not icy, and Ben soon got used to it. With Angelo alongside him, he kicked his way down, switching on the powerful underwater torch as they got too deep for the sun's light to penetrate fully. Instantly the ocean seemed to light up and a nearby shoal of brightly coloured fish swerved away from the sudden light in a single, graceful movement. Ben's ears were filled with the heavy sound of his own breath, and as he kicked even deeper he moved the torch around to try and find the bank of coral that he loved visiting so much.

It didn't take long to locate the complicated wall of colour that they were looking for. They approached it reverentially, as if they would scare it away if they were anything other than respectful. As they swam towards it, Ben saw the huge, flat form of a stingray. When he had first seen one of these strange, beautiful fish, he had been a bit fearful. But Angelo had explained that they rarely attacked human beings with their poisonous stinger, and Ben had learned to admire them at close range. The stingray drifted away and in its place another shoal of bright-yellow fish seemed to appear from nowhere. It was a beautiful sight, caught against the oranges and purples of the coral. Ben felt he could stay down there for ever.

Time never seemed to have any meaning under-water. It could have been half an hour or longer that they drifted around the coral bank, admiring the amazing range of sea creatures that congregated there. Ben knew that his oxygen wouldn't last more than an hour, though, so after a bit he decided, regretfully, that it was time to surface.

And it was at just that moment that he saw them.

They seemed to appear from nowhere – four divers, with bright beams and black wetsuits. Ben started, then quickly turned his head towards Angelo, who was also looking all around him, clearly surprised by the sudden company. Two of them were coming towards him and in the few seconds he had to look at their faces through the masks, Ben saw expressions of grim severity. Instinctively he kicked his flippers and tried to get away.

Immediately they were after him. From the corner of his eye, he could see that they had already grabbed Angelo, who seemed to be struggling. He wanted to go and help his friend, but what could he do against four fully-grown men? Indeed, what could he do against two of them – the two who were only metres behind him as he kicked as fast as he could and tried to get away? Panic surged through him. Who were they? What did they want? Shoals of fish flew out of his way as he forced the muscles in his legs to work hard, but it was no good. He felt the firm grip of a hand round his ankle. His body went into spasm as he tried to escape, but in seconds he was being firmly held by the two divers, who slowly started moving up towards the surface.

Ben's brain was working overtime, but there seemed no way he could escape. There wouldn't be much oxygen left in his canister and he knew that as he was struggling he was likely to be taking bigger breaths, which meant he could run out very soon. There was nothing for it but to see what these men wanted.

Suddenly the underwater silence was shattered by a roaring noise in his ears as they broke through the surface of the sea. Ben had only a couple of seconds to take everything in. It was so different to when they made the dive: the sky was grey and the sea, which had been calm and flat, was now angry and swelling. Angelo's boat was overturned, its hull bobbing up and down in the rough water. Then a wave hit Ben full in the face, blinding him momentarily and making him gasp for breath. When he emerged, he realized that the two divers had let go of him and the air was filled with their shouts. 'Get to the boat!' a voice called, full of urgency. *'Get to the boat!'*

Ben looked around. Just beyond Angelo's speedboat there was another vessel – larger, but still struggling in the billowing waves. It bobbed out of sight momentarily with the swell. *'The boat!'* a voice called again. A figure came into Ben's field of vision. It was one of the divers. He was close by. 'Ditch the gas,' the man shouted. 'Ditch it now! It's weighing you down!'

Ben found himself underwater again. He fumbled with the buckle that tied the air canisters to his body and was desperate to breathe by the time he got rid of them. It was easier to push himself up now. When he emerged again, he gulped hungrily at the air before hurling himself round the capsized boat and towards the bigger vessel.

He could see Angelo being pulled aboard, along with three of the other divers. Ben's muscles were burning with the effort; he felt weak. 'Keep going!' the voice called from behind him. Ben set his face into a grimace and urged himself forward.

It was dangerous approaching the boat – it seemed out of control, buffeted by the winds and the rough sea. Someone threw him a length of rope with a flotation ring tied to it. Ben only just managed to grab it before it was washed out of reach. He felt himself being pulled in. As he approached the boat a wave caught him and his face smashed against the side of the hull. It stung, but he grimly held onto the ring and slowly he was pulled up into the boat.

As soon as he was in, he felt his knees buckle. At the same time, the boat lurched. Ben fell awkwardly to the floor. *L182,929/Ya*

'Ben!' He heard Angelo's voice, but he couldn't see him. '*Il tuo viso! Stai sanguinando!* Your face, it is bleeding!' Ben touched his hand to his cheek, then looked at it. Blood. He had obviously cut himself when he hit the side of the boat.

The wind was screaming now, so loud that it almost drowned out the noise of the motor being started up.

Ben saw one more man – the helper who had been on board their small boat – being pulled up into the vessel before it suddenly moved away, crashing up and down through the billowing sea towards the shore. It was chaos on board – there seemed to be too many passengers for the small craft – and when Ben shouted he didn't really know who he was talking to.

'What's going on?' he screamed.

'Hurricane,' one of the men replied curtly. He had short-cropped blond hair, but as he was no longer wearing his mask, Ben couldn't tell if he was one of the guys who had grabbed him. ''Fraid you got whipped by the edge of it.'

'The edge of it?' Ben shouted. 'You mean the actual thing's worse?'

'Yeah, son. Much worse. This one came out of nowhere. Even the weather boys weren't expecting it. Good job we knew exactly where you were – your surface guy called it in, but you'd be fish food if we hadn't found you.'

Ben looked around and saw Angelo. His tanned face had gone pale and his long hair was stuck to his skin. As he gripped onto the side of the boat he looked shocked. Shocked and scared. Ben didn't blame him. One look at the state of the sea told him how lucky they had been.

'Sorry if we scared you down there,' the voice

continued. 'Wasn't really the time and place for proper introductions.'

'Forget about it,' Ben said shortly. He was more concerned about getting his feet on dry land.

They reached the shore with difficulty. Even in the shallow water it was difficult to wade out, and when Ben and Angelo finally got to the beach, they both collapsed on the sand while the frogmen who had rescued them ran off, no doubt to continue their life-guarding duties. Within seconds Angelo was surrounded by two bodyguards, who started talking to him in hushed voices. Ben tried to get some sense of what they were saying, but without success. It was only when Angelo stood up that he seemed to realize that Ben had no idea what was going on.

'There's a' – Angelo paused as he searched for the word – 'a hurricane. A bad one. It's approaching now. My father wants me off the island – there's a small charter flight leaving in half an hour to the US main-land. It takes off from the other side of the island. They think they can stay away from the danger area.' A serious expression crossed his face. 'He got a ticket on the plane for you too, if you want it. But we have to leave immediately.' He glanced at one of the body-guards, an enormous man with a square, unsmiling face. 'Brad's taking me to the airport now.'

Ben bit his lower lip. He didn't much fancy staying

here on the island, but as that thought crossed his mind, he glanced up the beach towards Alec's house. He didn't feel great about leaving the old man here to face the devastation to come, either. Ben jumped to his feet. 'I'll be two minutes,' he shouted.

He ripped off his flippers and hurtled up the beach, ignoring the way the wind stung his wet skin, up into Alec's garden. The old man was waiting for him in the porch. The moment he saw Ben, a look of relief crashed over his face. 'Bit blowy out there,' he said wryly.

'Yeah,' Ben replied breathlessly. 'You could say that. I just heard a hurricane's going to hit.'

If Alec was surprised or worried by the news, he didn't show it. He just nodded his head calmly. 'First I've heard of it,' he commented.

'Came out of nowhere, apparently. Angelo said he can get me off the island on the same flight as him.'

'Then you must go,' Alec replied. 'I'm sure you don't want to add this to your ever-growing list of disasters.' He winked mischievously.

'What about you? I could ask him if there's another seat on the plane.'

Alec smiled. 'Ben,' he said softly – so softly that he was difficult to hear over the sound of the screaming winds outside – 'listen. If only half of what you have told me about your exploits is true, you're a brave lad. A very brave lad. But you can't go round the world saving everyone, you know.' He looked out to sea. 'Besides, I've seen a few strong winds in my time. I think I'll just batten down the hatches and sit it out.' He looked back at Ben and winked. 'Go on,' he said. 'Get your things together. If you get off the island today, you can be back home tomorrow. And I don't think we need a long drawn-out goodbye, do you?'

It only took Ben a couple of minutes to change and stuff everything into his holdall. When he was ready he sprinted downstairs. Alec shook his hand. 'It's been nice to have you, Ben,' he said. 'Come and see me again soon, won't you?'

'You bet,' Ben replied.

'You should go, matey,' Alec said.

Ben nodded and made for the door. As he left, he looked back over his shoulder. Alec was staring out of the window, over the sea and to the boiling sky beyond. His wild hair was blowing in the wind and he seemed lost in thought. Ben left him to it.

Minutes later, he and Angelo were in a spacious Mercedes driven by the big bodyguard. As they sped away from the house, there was no reason for either of them to notice an altogether less impressive car pull into the road and follow them, keeping its distance, but being very, very careful not to lose them.

Chapter Two

'They are on flight GXR1689 bound for Miami, leaving from Gate 3.'

'You are sure?' The man ran his finger gently down the scar on the side of his face as he spoke – a habit of his.

'They will be boarding any minute.' The two men on either side of the telephone conversation were not speaking English, but some other language.

'And will you be on the flight with them?' the scarred man demanded quietly.

'I have the last seat.'

'Good. We are lucky. This storm was not expected. Let us hope that bringing our plans forward at the last minute does not ruin them.'

'You are nearby? You will be able to board the plane unnoticed?'

'I think so.' He continued to stroke his scar. 'But if I am unsuccessful, I wish you luck with our backup plan. Remember, we do this for the good of our people. Do not be scared.'

'I'm not scared. If death comes, I will embrace it.'

'As will I.'

The man pressed a button on his mobile phone and hung up.

He was not a big man, but he was stocky and strong. The scar down the left-hand side of his face was angry and red, and at that exact moment he stood at the edge of Grand Cayman airport, only metres away from an aircraft hangar. The sea was behind him. He had already cut a hole in the wire perimeter fence and he lost no time in clambering through it. He ran quickly to the hangar, then skirted around the outside until he found the entrance. It was there that he discovered what he was looking for: a member of the airport staff dressed in the regulation short-sleeved khaki uniform. He stepped into the worker's field of vision, then disappeared again behind the hangar.

'Hey!' the worker called. 'What are you doing there?' He followed the man suspiciously.

That was his big mistake.

It only took the man one blow on the back of the worker's neck to knock him unconscious, and as soon as the victim hit the ground he started to remove his clothes. They didn't fit him *that* well, but they would do. In under a minute he was indistinguishable from any of the other airport workers on site, other than the fact that he carried a small rucksack full of essential items. Essential to him, at least.

It was not a big airfield, and he could see Gate 3 less than 100 metres away. A small twin-propeller aircraft of the kind used for short hops was waiting there, its luggage being loaded. It was an old-fashioned-looking plane that had clearly been hauled into service to get people off the island before the storms hit. A few final passengers were walking across the tarmac and climbing up into the aircraft as he approached, but none of them paid him any attention. Nor did the two baggage handlers who were using a truck to reverse pallets of luggage up into the plane. He walked in the shadowof one of these pallets, completely unobserved, and up the ramp. Quickly, before anyone could notice him, he hid behind a pallet that was already loaded.

No one would see him here, he decided. When they were in the air he would have to work quickly – the temperature in the hold would soon drop. But for now he had to keep quiet.

He had to keep still.

He had to trust his luck, and wait until takeoff.

Ben didn't mind admitting to himself that he felt

nervous as he strapped himself firmly into his seat. He'd been in enough aeroplanes, of course, in his time; he'd even flown a microlight over Adelaide in some pretty hairy circumstances. But as he sat next to Angelo in their seats near the front of the plane – Angelo's bodyguard had taken a place in the seat behind them – he could already hear the wind outside. It wasn't as strong as it had been at the beach, but it was still – as Alec would have said – a bit blowy, and Ben knew that it was going to be a bumpy takeoff.

The plane was bound for Miami. It was a twin-propeller aircraft and the propellers had already been spinning as they were ushered onto it with the last few remaining passengers. Ben didn't know why, but there was something about a twin-prop plane that made him feel less safe than a jet plane. They looked out of date, somehow, and his mind wasn't put at rest by the interior of the aircraft either. He had the impression that this plane had been in service for a very long time. He put that thought from his mind: the pilot would know what he was doing. He wasn't going to risk his life and the lives of everyone else on board by taking off if he thought it was dangerous.

'Thanks for doing this,' he said to Angelo. 'Looking at the chaos back at the terminal, I reckon I'd have been lucky to get a flight this side of Christmas.'

Angelo looked a bit embarrassed. '*Di niente*,' he said

shortly. 'It's fine. There have to be some advantages to—' He stopped mid-sentence, as though he had caught himself saying something he didn't want to say. Instead, he glanced down the aisle of the plane. The last couple of passengers were boarding, bringing the total number of people on board this small plane up to about twenty or thirty. They took the last two remaining seats, one just near Ben and Angelo, the other much further back. 'Anyway,' Angelo continued, 'other people seem to have got seats. You would probably have been OK.'

Ben shrugged. 'Maybe,' he said, as the gentle hum of the engines became a little louder. A voice came over the speakers and the cabin crew performed their safety announcement as the plane trundled towards the runway. It turned, paused for a moment and then the engines started to scream. The plane accelerated, Ben was pushed back in his seat and moments later they were airborne.

He hadn't been wrong about the bumpy takeoff – it was a bit like being in the boat earlier on. The winds buffeted the plane, knocking it from side to side and making the whole aircraft shudder. Ben found that he was gripping his armrests, white-knuckled, and when he glanced over at Angelo, he saw that his friend had gone rather pale.

'It's fine,' Angelo said, though he sounded more like

he was reassuring himself than Ben. 'We need to get above the winds. I've been on lots of bumpy fl—'

He didn't finish his sentence, because the plane performed a horrible lurch, then seemed to drop from the sky momentarily before continuing its ascent.

'It'll be fine,' Angelo breathed again. Ben just closed his eyes and waited for the shaking to stop.

It took about five minutes for the flight to settle down, although it seemed like a lot longer to Ben. Still, it was a real relief when it happened. He and Angelo gave each other a sheepish smile. Neither of them, he sensed, wanted to admit how much the takeoff had frightened them.

'Where are you headed after you get to Miami?' Ben asked. The plane tilted as he spoke, and the sun shone directly into their eyes.

'To Italy,' Angelo replied. 'Back home.' He didn't sound too thrilled by the idea.

'Yeah, it's home for me too.' Ben smiled. 'Worst luck.'

Angelo looked at him and then spoke in a con-spiratorial whisper. 'It's not so bad for you,' he breathed, and pointed his thumb back towards the seat his bodyguard had taken. 'You don't have people like him following you all the time.'

Ben had to admit that it didn't sound great being under someone's watchful gaze every waking moment, but he tried to cheer Angelo up. 'It can't be that bad,' he said a bit weakly. 'At least you know you're, er, safe and everything.'

Angelo snorted. 'Safe from what?' he asked. Ben didn't have an answer to that question.

They had been flying for about twenty minutes when the captain announced over the loudspeaker that they had reached their cruising altitude. All signs of the turbulence they had encountered at takeoff had disappeared now, and the ride was smooth. Angelo's bodyguard stood up and walked a little way up and down the aisle. He walked nonchalantly, as if he was simply stretching his legs, but the dark look Angelo cast him suggested to Ben that the guy was doing a little more than that. Clearly he was satisfied that everything was all right, however, because he soon sat down again, winking at the two of them – a bit patronizingly, Ben thought – before he did so.

'Does he really follow you *everywhere*?' Ben whispered.

Angelo nodded his head. 'There are three of them,' he confided. 'They take it in turns.'

'But why?' Ben asked.

Angelo inclined his head slightly. '*I soldi*. Money. My father is a very wealthy man. Wealthy men can be paranoid. He thinks I am at risk of being . . .' He paused for a moment, searching for the word.

'Kidnapped,' he said finally. 'He thinks I will be kidnapped and held for ransom. Me, I think it is stupid. Only famous people get kidnapped.'

Ben wasn't so sure that that was true. He kept his mouth shut, though: it was clearly a sore point for Angelo. Instead he settled back in his seat and felt his eyes becoming heavy. He had slept badly the night before, and it had already been an eventful day. After a few moments he nodded off to sleep.

The temperature was dropping in the hold, and fast. The man's body was bruised and sore from the way he had been thrown around during the bumpy takeoff, but he put all thoughts of that from his mind. He clambered his way to the front of the plane, climbing over the pallets of luggage as he went. Before long he came to a metal panel sealed along the side with a number of tightly wound screws.

Quickly he opened his rucksack and pulled out an electric screwdriver. It was difficult to keep his grip true down here, but the screws unwound quickly enough. In a couple of minutes he was able to pull the metal panel away. He clambered into the small chamber that he could tell, from the rounded shape of the plane's nose, was just below the cockpit.

It was freezing now, but the aircraft was still climbing. He looked above and saw the trap door that led into the cockpit. He would not break through it yet. Not just yet. He would wait a little longer. Wait until the cold became unbearable. By that time, he hoped, the aircraft would be fully on course.

Only then, he decided, would it begin.

It was the sudden, clunky juddering that woke Ben up – a juddering that felt as if someone had taken the plane in their hands and given it a good shake. It felt like they had done the same to Ben's stomach too. And then there were the screams – the screams and the horrible sensation of the aircraft going into freefall.

'What's happening?' he shouted as, terrified, he gripped on firmly to the arms of his seat. '*What's happening?*'

The cabin crew had been hurled to the floor at the back by the sudden change in the plane's movement. Ben thought that one of the screams came from an air stewardess – never a good sign. He looked out of the window, half expecting to see the bubbling skies of the hurricane they were escaping. But he didn't. All he saw was clear blue.

When your plane is going down, time has no meaning. It couldn't have been more than about twenty seconds that they stayed like that, but it seemed like half a lifetime. Half a lifetime of cold, blind terror. Suddenly, though, Ben felt the plane straighten up, and the popping in his ears told him that they were gaining height again. He exhaled deeply with relief, and he could sense Angelo doing the same.

'What's going on?' he breathed. 'What was that?'

Angelo shook his head, but he still seemed too scared to speak. The bodyguard, on the other hand, immediately got to his feet. He said something to Angelo in curt Italian. Angelo nodded.

'What happened?' Ben demanded, not at all sure that the bodyguard spoke any English.

'I don't know,' the burly man replied in a perfect American accent that slightly surprised Ben.

'Something to do with the hurricane?'

'Looks bright and sunny outside to me,' the bodyguard growled. 'Stay where you are. I'll go and find out.' He stepped out into the aisle and walked down to the crew.

Ben and Angelo watched them intently, but from this distance it was impossible to tell what they were saying or what was happening. After a while, Ben couldn't hack it any more. They should have heard something from the captain by now. His silence was worrying. With a determined look on his face Ben unbuckled his seatbelt and pushed past Angelo. 'I'm going to find out what's happening,' he said, before walking down to the rear, ignoring the stares of the other passengers, who obviously wanted to do the same thing but were too scared to unbuckle themselves.

'What's going on?' he demanded of the worried-looking cabin crew.

One of the air stewards – a tall man with perfectly groomed dark hair and a cheesy smile – answered. 'Nothing to worry about, son,' he said. 'Take your seat, please.'

But Ben didn't take his seat. He wasn't going to be fobbed off like that. He turned to the bodyguard. 'Have you found out what's happening?' he demanded.

For a moment the bodyguard hesitated, as if he was in two minds whether to tell Ben or not. When he finally spoke, he was tense and serious. 'There is an intercom between the cabin and the cockpit,' he said quietly. 'They've been trying to buzz through to the pilot to find out what went on up there, but there's no reply.'

Ben's brow furrowed. 'Can't we just open the door?'

The air steward shook his head. 'Can't be done,' he said. 'Since 9/11, no aircraft cockpits can be entered from the cabin.'

'How many pilots are there?' Ben asked.

'Two.'

'And neither of them are replying?'

The air steward shook his head again.

'What are we going to do?'

The man gave Ben a patronizing smile. '*We*,' he said

emphatically, 'are not going to do anything. *You* are going to take your seat and keep quiet about all this. The last thing we need is any more panic in the cabin, OK.'

Ben glanced over his shoulder back at the terrified passengers. 'I think that might be asking a bit much,' he murmured. As he spoke, the air steward took him by the shoulders, turned him round and gave him a little shove back towards his seat.

But Ben never got there, because just as he started up the aisle, the loudspeaker crackled into life.

'Ladies and gentleman,' an unfamiliar voice announced in an accent Ben did not recognize. 'I advise you all to remain very calm. This plane has been hijacked and is under my control. I will be giving you instructions very soon. In the meantime, be assured that if anyone tries to enter the cockpit or tamper with its door, they will immediately be shot.'

With that, the loudspeaker went dead.

There was a brief moment of silence, and then the sound of panicked screams filled the aircraft.

Chapter Three

It was only fair, the hijacker thought to himself, that the passengers should know why they were going to die before it happened.

Beside him, the two pilots lay dead. They had shouted in surprise as the hijacker emerged through the trap door, but two silent, accurate shots from his suppressed weapon – a Beretta 92FS that he had stashed in his rucksack – had floored them before they could raise the alarm. It had been a nasty surprise when the plane had veered out of control – he had expected there to be an autopilot, but clearly they had been flying manually. Only with difficulty had he managed to take the pilot's seat and steady the plane. Now his eyes were scanning over the bewildering array of instruments before him. It took a couple of minutes for him to work out what was what – he had only ever flown much simpler aircraft than this before – but eventually he felt comfortable with it. He breathed deeply and calmly as his body warmed up.

Looking out over the sea and sky that stretched before him, he felt a sense of peace, as though the whole world was his. He was lucky to have got this far, and now there was really nothing that could stop him from doing what he had to do. Even if he didn't hit his target, he would be able to ensure a successful outcome. He would be able to make sure the plane went down. But for now he could just sit here. The aircraft was on course and he didn't need to do anything. Not yet. Let the passengers calm down first, and then he would tell them what the future held.

Yes, he thought to himself once more. It was only fair that they should know why they were going to die before it happened.

The moment the hijacker had made his announcement, the whole cabin had dissolved into chaos.

All the passengers were standing up now, and some of them had rushed into the aisle. Ben's ears were filled with shouting and crying – the sound of panic and distress. The cabin staff were shouting too, trying to get everyone to sit down, to remain calm. But they didn't seem to be having any effect.

Ben felt the big hand of the bodyguard on his

shoulder. When he spoke, his voice was quietly reassuring, but firm. 'You need to go and sit with Angelo. Try and keep calm.'

Ben didn't move. There were too many unanswered questions in his mind. 'If the cockpit door is locked,' he asked, 'how did anyone get in there?'

'I don't know,' replied the bodyguard. He looked just as confused as Ben.

'You think it's one of the pilots?'

They were interrupted by the air steward. 'It's not a pilot,' he said breathlessly. 'I know them both well. I'd recognize the voice.'

'This plane's going to Miami. What will the Americans do?' Ben asked. 'If they realize we've been hijacked, I mean.'

The bodyguard and the air steward gave each other a meaningful glance, but they didn't answer. 'Go and sit down, son,' Ben was told. 'Leave this to us.'

Ben thought of arguing, but in the end he did as he was told. As he worked his way back up to his seat, he noticed that most of the passengers had also sat down, but there was still the noise of terrified voices in the air. Ben wondered how long it would be before the panic gripped them again. Not very, probably.

Angelo was ashen-faced. 'Do you think this is because of me?' he asked immediately as Ben pushed past him to take his seat.

'How can it be?' Ben replied. 'You weren't even meant to be on this plane.'

Angelo furrowed his brow and nodded. 'I suppose so,' he muttered, but something in his voice suggested he wasn't convinced. 'Do you think we're going to die?'

Ben glanced out of the window. It was a question he'd been asking himself. For a moment he didn't answer; he just stared into the blue of the sea thousands of feet below. He took a deep, determined breath, then looked back at Angelo. 'No,' he said firmly. 'Trust me. I've been in risky situations before. We're not going to die. We're probably just going to be used for ransom and—'

'I think we are going to die,' Angelo interrupted. He was breathing nervously, in short gasps. 'Think about it, Ben. As soon as the Americans know the plane has been hijacked, they will blow us from the sky. They won't want another 9/11 on their hands.'

Ben blinked. He remembered how the bodyguard and air steward had avoided answering his question. Now he knew why. He tried to think of an argument against Angelo's nightmare scenario, but he couldn't.

'I don't think we've gone off course yet,' he said. 'No one will know anything's wrong unless they try to make radio contact with the pilot. But even then, the hijacker might be able to bluff it.' He took a deep breath. 'We have to do something before this guy changes direction.'

As Ben spoke, the bodyguard approached. His face was grim as he knelt down in the aisle. 'I'm going to try something,' he said. 'Now listen to me, you two. No heroics, OK?'

'What are you going to do?' Angelo asked.

The bodyguard's eyes flickered towards the cockpit, then back to the two of them. 'I'm wearing a bullet-proof vest,' he said. 'It'll absorb most rounds at close range. I'm going to call his bluff, try and knock the door in. Maybe he really does have a gun, maybe not. But if he opens it, I reckon I should be good to over-power him. If not' – he tapped on his chest – 'I came well dressed for the job of taking a bullet.'

'But what if he—' Ben started to say, but the body-guard interrupted him.

'Trust me,' he said. 'I'm trained for this.' He smiled at both of them. 'You OK?'

Ben and Angelo nodded. 'Aren't you going to let everyone else know?' Ben asked.

The bodyguard shook his head. 'Too risky,' he said.

'What do you mean? Why?'

The man glanced down the aisle. 'We don't know for sure that the guy in the cockpit's the only one. It would be unusual for a hijacker to act alone.'

'You mean—' Ben and Angelo looked at each other.

'You mean, someone in the cabin could be working with them?'

The bodyguard shrugged. 'It's possible. There's even a chance one of the cabin crew is involved. We need to be careful, guys. Very careful. Don't trust anyone, not unless they prove themselves to be trustworthy. OK?'

'OK,' Ben and Angelo said in unison.

The bodyguard nodded, then stood up and walked the few rows up towards the front.

'You think he's up to it?' Ben asked Angelo in a low whisper, keeping his voice quiet so that nobody else would hear them talking.

Angelo nodded seriously. 'Brad used to be in Delta Force. He doesn't talk about it much, but from what I can tell he's been all over the world with them. Anti-terrorism mostly.' He looked a bit rueful. 'I always thought that looking after spoiled rich kids like me was a bit of a come-down for him. Guess I was wrong. Still, if anyone can sort this situation out, I think it is him.' He smiled nervously. 'I asked him once how many men he had killed.'

'What did he say?'

'He said, "How do you know they were all men?" I think he was joking, though.'

Ben found it hard to laugh. His mouth had gone dry, he realized, and his body felt weak. He was cold, but he was still sweating. Ben Tracey knew what fear felt like, and he was feeling it now. Brad might be highly trained, but his plan didn't sound that great to him. Not that Ben could think of anything better. They just had to hope that the bodyguard's special forces training hadn't deserted him.

Ben craned his neck to look over the seat in front. At the front of the aisle he could see Brad preparing himself. All around the plane the buzz of panicked voices was rising again. He could hear people trying to make calls on their mobile phones, but there was no signal this high up and they were left shouting pointlessly into their handsets. Ben didn't get the sense that any of them were paying much attention to Brad.

All that was about to change though.

When the bodyguard hurled his heavy shoulder against the door, it made a dull thud but didn't seem to make much difference to the entrance. A few people around him fell quiet. Brad stepped back and then made another run. By the time he hit the door for a second time, everyone in the plane seemed to know what he was doing.

'What's going on?' one man at the back shouted. 'Don't be an idiot!'

But Brad ignored him. He stepped back again, set his shoulders and then started running towards the door for a third time.

And it was only then that the plane nosedived yet again . . .

In the cockpit, the first bump on the door had made the hijacker jump.

The man spun round. His eyes were narrow and his fist gripped the gun firmly.

There was a pause, and then a second bump. The door shook slightly, but it held fast. He eyed the locking mechanism – a big red handle at the twelve o'clock position with an arrow pointing downwards. To open the door, all he needed to do was pull it down.

He checked the gun. It was loaded and ready. He would have to be fast. Fast and accurate. When he let go of the controls, the plane would dive. But that would be OK, just as long as he was expecting it. He took a deep breath and let go of the controls. Immediately the plane tilted downwards and he had to hurl himself towards the door. With one hand he held the gun out straight; with the other he brought down the locking handle and pulled the door open.

The hijacker only had a split second to take everything in. Barely a metre away from him there was a large, thick-set man, and he was coming towards him at some speed.

Their eyes locked. The hijacker aimed the gun straight at his head.

He fired.

The force of the bullet knocked the man backwards.

There was no way the hijacker's target would have survived the headshot, but the man fired once more for good measure. This time the bullet hit the bodyguard in the chest.

The hijacker slammed the door shut and forced the locking lever up again. Sweat was trickling down the side of his face now, but he remained calm as he carefully edged himself towards his seat again, grabbed the controls and steadied the plane.

Three people dead. But that didn't matter. It was only a matter of time before it happened to all of them.

Chapter Four

It sounded like everyone started screaming at the same time. The plane had nosedived and it was that which was scaring everyone, rather than the silent bullets. As he gripped fearfully onto his seat, Ben wondered how many people had even noticed that the bodyguard had been shot.

One person had, though. Angelo.

'*Brad!*' The Italian boy's yell filled Ben's ears. As the plane suddenly pulled out of its dive and started rising again, Angelo rushed into the aisle and up to the body lying on the floor. Ben followed immediately.

'Stay away, you two!' one of the cabin crew shouted, but he was quickly rebuked by Angelo.

'*Stai zitto!*' the Italian said between gritted teeth. 'Shut up! Brad was here because of me, all right?' But when he came up close to the corpse, Ben noticed that his friend took a step back.

The bodyguard was a mess. His face was bloodied and unrecognizable, and half of his head had been shot away. It was a gruesome sight.

As he stared at the bodyguard's corpse, the noise of frightened people all around him seemed to disappear into nothing. Ben had seen enough dead bodies in his time, but it wasn't something he'd got used to. The sight of Brad, dead and cold, sent a shiver down his spine and made him feel sick.

It was only the sound of the intercom crackling into life again that snapped him out of it. Everyone else in the cabin fell silent too as the hijacker's voice filled the air.

'Ladies and gentlemen.' His foreign voice sounded almost polite. 'I advise you all to take your seats and remain calm.'

Ben felt as if everyone in the cabin was holding their breath. All he could hear was the sound of the plane's engines.

'If anybody else tries to do anything foolish,' the hijacker continued, 'they can expect to die, like the man I have just shot.'

There were some shocked whispers from the back of the plane – clearly not everybody had been aware that Brad had been shot.

'It seems fair to me,' the hijacker continued, 'that you understand what is going to happen to you *before* it happens. And why.'

A pause. A deathly silence.

'I come from a small island many thousands of miles from here. I do not believe any of you will have heard of it. You are all too caught up in the importance of your own affairs to worry about people like us. Not long ago, men from the West invaded our island. They were not an army, and no doubt news of the invasion did not reach your ears; but to my people their arrival was a terrible event. They raped our land in their search for oil; and because of their greed, our children have started to die.'

The hijacker's voice was flat and emotionless now. Ben thought he could sense a tone of determination. In the cabin, the silence had turned into a hum of curious voices. There was still an atmosphere of thick fear, but the hijacker had certainly got their attention. Ben turned to Angelo. His Italian friend's face was expressionless as he continued to listen to the words coming over the intercom.

'I myself witnessed a father carrying the body of his daughter out of their house. She was killed by the machines of the men who thoughtlessly ravaged our island in their search for oil. The world did not hear about the little girl's death, but what we will do today will set that right. Today we will avenge the death of an innocent. Today my people will stand up to the invaders.'

As he spoke, the hijacker's expressionless voice became almost excited. Ben didn't know what their enemy looked like, but in his head he pictured a face that was beaming fanatically.

'We are headed towards the southern tip of Florida,' the hijacker continued, his voice slightly calmer now. 'The oil company that did us this injustice owns a large refinery there. This plane will act like a noble bullet. When it crashes into the refinery, the whole world will learn of the evils of the men who kill our children.'

It was the word 'crash' that did it, that sent the panic of the cabin into overdrive. Ben's ears were filled once more with the sound of people screaming, and he didn't blame them. He felt like screaming too. A deathly chill was running through his veins and it was all he could do to stop himself from collapsing, sick with fear. He grabbed onto the back of the nearest seat.

'I estimate that we are half an hour away from our target.' Ben had to strain now to hear the hijacker's voice above the noise of the cabin. 'I do not intend to speak to you again, but I suggest you use the time to consider the evils the Western world has inflicted upon us, and the part you have played in it.'

And then, as suddenly as it had started, the crackle of the intercom disappeared.

* * *

The air-traffic control tower of Miami International Airport throbbed with activity.

The hurricane in the Caribbean Sea had come from nowhere and it was moving fast – a freak of nature that was as unpredictable as it was unexpected. Already it had hit the Cayman Islands, leaving a trail of un-believable devastation in its wake, and they'd nearly lost a 747 that had strayed too close to the headwinds. All the controllers in the control tower had sweat on their brows as they stared at their bank of computer screens, intently watching the flight paths of the planes that were being diverted round the area. Each aircraft on the screen was accompanied by a string of information – the flight number, the type of plane, its altitude and direction. It was a lot to take in, and you needed your wits about you.

Jack Simpson was twenty-five years old and he hadn't been in the job long. Not long enough to feel entirely confident. But as he spoke to the pilots he was guiding into the area, he did his best not to let any nervousness show in his voice. He knew that was the last thing pilots wanted to hear, especially in a difficult, high-traffic situation like this. And so he kept his voice calm as five passenger jets circled in a holding pattern to the east of Miami, and a good many more approached across his screen.

'Hurricane's heading north!' he heard someone in the room shout. There was a murmur among everyone there. They all knew what that meant: it was heading their way. Jack did his best not to think about his mother, living alone in a retirement village on the coast. She'd been battered by enough high winds in the past few years. If this one didn't break up before it hit land, she'd be battered by another. Jack wasn't sure she had it in her. He winced as he tried to put that thought from his head. He had to concentrate on the job in hand, and that job was to make sure these planes landed safely.

As Jack stared at the screen, however, something caught his attention. A flashing light on the screen – one of the aircraft. His eyebrows crumpled as he looked at it: the plane seemed to be losing height. And fast.

'You see that, Jack?' his colleague sitting next to him asked tensely.

'Yeah,' Jack replied. 'I see it.'

And then, suddenly, the aircraft appeared to stop losing height and to start climbing again.

The two air-traffic controllers glanced at each other, worried looks on their faces. 'Better make contact,' Jack said, and his colleague nodded.

Jack checked the flight number of the aircraft – GXR1689 from Grand Cayman to Miami International – and the frequency of its communication system. Within seconds he was trying to get through to the plane's pilot.

'Flight GXR1689, this is Miami International. Do you read me? Over.'

Jack waited for a reply. There was none. Just an empty crackle. He cast his colleague another worried look. 'Flight GXR1689, this is Miami International. Do you read me? Over.'

Nothing.

Jack took a deep breath. Total radio silence from an approaching civilian aircraft. This was the sort of thing that only happened in training exercises. But this was no exercise. Something was going on with this plane. It could be in trouble. Or it could be about to *cause* trouble. Either way, if there was no response from the cockpit, there was only one course of action.

Jack knew what to do. He knew he had to raise the alarm.

He picked up a telephone handset. 'Inform the Department of Homeland Security,' he said curtly. 'We've got a Code Red.'

Ben felt like he was frozen to the spot. The sight of the bodyguard's dead body did not affect him now; all the emotions he might have felt had been replaced with blind dread. It took a supreme effort for him to turn to look at Angelo. When he did, he received quite a shock.

His friend's tortured face spoke of a million different emotions, none of them good. Between gritted teeth, the Italian boy spoke. '*Ben*,' he hissed. '*I need to talk to you. Now!*'

Ben nodded. The two of them headed back to their seats, fighting their way through a scramble of people trying to look at Brad's corpse. Once they were sitting down again, Angelo spoke in a hushed, urgent whisper.

'I told you,' he said. 'I told you it was my fault.'

Ben looked at him in confusion. 'Your fault? What do you mean, it's your fault?'

'My father,' Angelo insisted. 'The oil refinery the hijacker was talking about – my father owns it. That's why they have chosen this plane.'

Ben stared at his friend. 'You know what?' he breathed. 'This is turning into a really bad day.' He took a deep breath and furrowed his brow. 'But it still doesn't make sense. How did they know you'd be on this flight?'

Angelo shrugged impatiently. '*Non so*. I don't know. How does anyone know anything?' he demanded. 'Maybe they have been watching me. Following me.'

'Or maybe,' Ben replied slowly, 'it's just a coincidence.'

Angelo snorted. 'Some coincidence. But listen, you can't tell anyone, OK? If the people on the plane find out, who knows what they'll do to me?'

Ben nodded. Angelo was right. The people around

them were panicking. The chances of them acting rationally and sensibly were small.

He glanced up the aisle to where a small group had congregated around Brad's dead body. They seemed to be arguing about something. Ben turned back to Angelo. 'To be honest,' he said, 'if we don't do something quick, it's not going to matter *who* your dad is – we're all going to be history in half an hour anyway.'

'But what can we do?' Angelo asked in panic, his voice wavering. 'He's got a gun . . . he's locked in there . . . he's—'

'*Calm down, Angelo!*' Ben hissed. 'Just calm down, all right? Let me think.'

Ben fell silent and tried to work his way through their options. It didn't help that Angelo was looking at him, his eyes wide with terror and his body shaking. And it didn't help, either, that Ben's mind didn't want to work. It was frozen by fear.

He closed his eyes and tried to concentrate.

There had to be a way out of this.

There *had* to be.

'Flight GXR1689, this is Miami International. Do you read me? Over.'

The hijacker stared at the radio. His lip curled. For a brief moment he thought about answering the call, but he quickly decided not to.

'*Flight GXR1689, this is Miami International. Do you read me? Over.*'

He stared resolutely at the instruments in front of him. Inwardly, he cursed. He had hoped to be able to get closer to the target before they contacted him. Now the alert would have been raised. There was a good chance that the military would be called in, and that before long he'd have US attack planes flying alongside him. The moment he started going off course, and if they couldn't identify the nature of the threat, they'd shoot him down. But maybe, just maybe, if he increased his airspeed and headed straight for the refinery now, he'd have a chance.

Decision made. He altered the throttle setting and reduced the drag on the wings. He watched in satis-faction as the instruments before him showed a substantial increase in velocity, and then he manoeuvred the control stick to head towards the coordinates he wanted.

Not long now, he told himself calmly.

Just hold your nerve and it won't be long now.

Ben opened his eyes suddenly. There had been a lurch in the aircraft's movements, as though they had suddenly increased their speed. Angelo had clearly noticed it too: his face had gone from pale to ghostly white.

Further up the aisle, the voices of the group of

people standing around Brad's body had grown louder. Ben stood up. 'Let's find out what's happening,' he said. 'See if anyone else has any bright ideas.' They stepped hurriedly into the aisle.

Two passengers, both men, were arguing. They were both tall and broad-shouldered, with bulging stomachs and American accents, though one was a good deal older than the other. They were both sweating profusely. 'He must have been in the hold,' the older man said. 'He *must* have been. How else could he get into the cockpit?'

'He can't have been,' the other one replied. 'The hold's depressurized. Takeoff would have killed him.'

'Not necessarily,' Ben interrupted, remembering something he'd learned at school. 'Aircraft holds are often pressurized. The only problem would have been the cold. It'll be freezing down there.'

The two men looked at him and blinked, as if surprised that someone as young as Ben might know more than them. 'Whatever, kid,' the younger man said dismissively. 'Bottom line is we're done for. This nutcase is taking the plane down, and we're going with him.'

The group fell silent. Some of them nodded their heads in agreement.

'So that's it, is it?' Ben demanded. 'We just sit here and let it happen?'

'None of us want to, son,' the older of the two men

told him. 'But it doesn't look to us like we've got a whole load of options. Try and break through to the cockpit and we get shot; go through the hold and we freeze to death, and if we don't we still get shot.'

Ben looked at them each in turn, amazed that they seemed to have given up so quickly. 'But – we've got to do *something*,' he announced. 'If we're all going to die anyway, surely anything's worth a try.' He realized he was shouting slightly. 'Come on – better for one of us to get shot than for all of us to burn to death in some oil refinery!'

'Look, son,' the older man continued. 'You're scared, and that's OK. But unless you've got any better ideas, the best thing we can all do is keep calm.'

Better ideas? Ben took a deep breath and looked around. Everyone's eyes seemed to be on him now, and he sensed that they were all waiting for him to come up with something. As he looked around, his eyes fell on the damaged corpse of Angelo's bodyguard, lying motionless in a pool of his own blood.

The man had asked for better ideas, and Ben realized that he was talking to him again in a somewhat hysterical voice. 'So have you, son? *Have you?*'

Ben looked up at him and a whisper of a smile played across his lips.

'Actually,' he said quietly, stepping forward towards Brad's body, 'I have.'

Chapter Five

Everyone went quiet, waiting for Ben to explain.

'Look,' he said, slightly breathlessly. 'The hijacker is obviously worried that we'll be able to break the door in if we try. That's why he shot Brad. So it's obvious, isn't it? Either we *do* break the door down, or we get him to open it himself.'

'But he's got a gun,' one of the group said, as though speaking to someone of below normal intelligence.

'Yeah, but Brad's got a bulletproof vest.'

'And that did him a lot of good,' the older man said, not hiding the scorn in his voice. 'Look, kid, if you haven't got anything sensible to add—'

'Wait,' Ben said impatiently. 'Think about it. If we barge the door again and the hijacker opens up to shoot, what part of the body is he going to go for?'

The group looked at each other, like a bunch of children in a classroom who weren't sure they knew the answer to a teacher's question. The voice that finally replied came from behind Ben.

'The head,' it said, clearly and confidently.

Ben spun round and he sensed everyone else in the group looking at this newcomer. The man standing behind them was tall and well tanned with dark, slicked-back hair. He looked South American maybe, and his accent was American too.

'Exactly,' Ben replied. 'So we need to remove the bulletproof vest and whoever barges the door has to hold it in front of their face.'

Another silence. A long one.

'You're mad,' a woman said, and there was a murmur of agreement.

Ben felt himself getting angry. 'Well, has anyone got any better ideas? Or shall we just sit around and wait to be blown up?'

More silence. And then the older man spoke. 'It's got to be worth a try,' he murmured.

'Yeah,' someone else agreed. 'It's not like we've got many options.'

'I think it's a very good idea,' the newcomer said firmly. He stepped forward and offered Ben his hand. 'My name's Danny.'

Ben shook his hand briefly. 'I'm Ben.'

'So who's going to perform this act of bravery then, Ben?'

None of the older people answered, but that was OK. Ben had it all worked out. 'It makes sense for the smallest person to do it,' he said. 'That way the bullet-proof vest will cover more of their body when they hold it up.' He looked around. He was quite a bit smaller than all the other adults. 'I'll do it,' he said firmly.

'And what happens,' Danny asked, 'if we overcome the hijacker? Does anyone here know how to fly a plane?'

Again, silence.

'Well, actually,' Ben said quietly, 'I kind of do. I mean, not a real plane like this, but I've flown a microlight before. I reckon I can keep it steady at least, and if we can get radio contact with Miami, maybe they can talk me through it, guide us down.' He glanced at everyone. They were all looking at him expectantly. 'Come on,' Ben said brusquely. 'We need to roll Brad's body over, unstrap the vest.'

It was Danny who bent down to help him. The bodyguard was quite a weight, and they really had to put their back into turning him over. As they did so, Ben tried not to look at the messed-up remains of his head. Danny ripped Brad's shirt open. Sure enough, beneath the torn material was a thick black bulletproof vest. The buckles were tight – they hurt Ben's fingers as he grappled with them – but a minute or so later they had undone the vest and rolled Brad back over. Ben moved his arms out so that they could take it off more easily.

When he stood up, he had the bulletproof vest in his hands. He was just holding it up in front of his body when he heard Angelo speak.

'Ben,' the Italian boy said firmly. '*Dammelo*. Give it to me.'

Ben blinked.

'I mean it, Ben. I'm slightly smaller than you, and if this goes according to plan, you don't want to be fighting the hijacker when you should be getting to the controls of the cockpit. And anyway, this *should* be my job.'

'Why?' a woman's voice asked.

Angelo didn't reply. He just stared meaningfully at Ben, who nodded slowly and handed the vest over to Angelo.

'All right, Angelo,' he said softly. 'If that's what you want.'

The two of them turned to look at the cockpit door. Ben couldn't help noticing that everyone had got out of their way and had retreated to the safety of their seats. Only Danny was standing with them.

Ben took a deep breath. Now was the time. The safety of everyone on the plane was up to them.

* * *

The two striker aircraft – Lockheed Martin F-35 Lightning IIs – had taken off from Key West Naval Air Station within minutes of the Code Red being raised. They roared from their island base out over the sea before making a sharp turn and heading through the clear sky up towards their target. Each of the aircraft carried easily enough weaponry to take down a civilian plane in mid-air, and both of them were flown by experienced pilots. Pilots who had been in war zones. Pilots who weren't afraid to carry out difficult orders if the chain of command made them.

The two F-35s appeared immediately on Jack Simpson's air-traffic control screen. These military aircraft were a different colour to the civilian planes that filled his screen. They moved faster too. Much faster. It was difficult to estimate these things, but Jack reckoned it wouldn't be more than ten minutes before they caught up with the rogue plane. What happened then would be anyone's guess. He felt his sweat seeping through all the pores of his skin as he tried to keep tabs on all the other air traffic and do his bit to guide them in safely. But it wasn't easy to concentrate when things were going so wrong up there. He wanted to close his eyes and pray for the poor passengers on the plane whose lives were hanging by a thread. But closing his eyes wouldn't have been sensible at all.

'Weird kind of day,' Jack's colleague observed. The guy's voice was tense.

'You can say that again,' Jack replied.

A pause as they both looked at their screens.

'They're calling it Hurricane Jasmine,' Jack's colleague continued.

'Pretty name,' Jack said.

'Not such a pretty storm.'

A voice shouted in the background. 'Listen up, everyone. All Florida airports to be closed to incoming traffic. Hurricane's moving quickly and unpredictably. Divert everything up north to Atlanta or Cincinnati.'

Jack's colleague snorted. 'Wouldn't mind being diverted up north myself. It's looking nasty out there.'

'We're safe here, aren't we?' Jack asked.

'Should be. Hurricane should pass to the west of here. Thing's got a mind of its own, though, so don't take my word for it.'

But Jack wasn't paying attention to him any more. He was staring again at the two striker planes moving inexorably towards the civilian aircraft.

It was just a communications failure, he told himself. Just that. Jack ignored the fact that the plane had changed course and increased its velocity. That was just a blip, surely. Maybe the pilot had been spooked by the approaching hurricane. Jack knew he would be.

But if the aircraft had maintained its original course, it would have landed well before the hurricane hit.

He put all those thoughts from his head. Any second, the radio frequency would burst into life and the military aircraft could pull away.

It was all going to be OK. Surely it was.

The bulletproof vest, opened up and held sideways, covered Angelo's head, his body and the top part of his legs.

'You ready?' Ben asked tersely.

'Ready,' Angelo replied. He was staring straight ahead of him and chewing his lower lip.

'OK,' Ben said. 'Listen carefully. I'm going to stand right behind you. We'll approach the door together and when we're there, you need to start kicking on it. Do it as hard as you can – it's really got to sound like we're trying to break the door down if we're going to persuade the hijacker to do something about it.'

Angelo nodded mutely.

'The plane's going to nosedive again the moment he lets go of the controls,' Ben continued. 'You need to be ready for it. Whatever you do, and whatever happens, you need to keep your head covered, OK?'

'OK.'

'I'll tell you when the door opens. Soon as it does, we charge him. If we get the right element of surprise,

63

we might be able to knock him down before he even fires.'

Angelo turned to Ben and smiled weakly. 'Nothing like being optimistic,' he said.

Ben grinned. 'I find it works for me,' he replied. 'Come on, let's go.'

There was absolute silence in the cabin as Ben and Angelo stepped forward. Ben could sense Angelo's anxiety, which only made the nerves he himself was feeling ten times worse. His hands were shaking and he couldn't get rid of the horrible sensation that he was only moments away from his own death.

'Good luck, Ben,' Angelo murmured.

'You too,' he whispered back. 'OK. Go for it!'

BANG! Angelo kicked the cockpit door with all his strength. He did it once, twice, a third time. The door rattled slightly.

'Keep going!' Ben told him. 'Keep kicking the door!'

Angelo's kicks became regular. As they continued, Ben noticed that his Italian friend had inadvertently lowered the bulletproof vest. The top of his head was peeking out above it. From behind, he yanked Angelo's arms. 'Keep it up,' he hissed. 'Keep the vest up.'

Angelo covered his face again. But as he did, the plane dipped.

Everyone in the cabin screamed again. Everyone, that is, except Ben and Angelo. They were expecting it, and they knew what it meant. 'He's coming!' Ben shouted. They both fell against the cockpit door, which suddenly opened.

It all happened so quickly. Ben heard the sound of the bullets this time as he was close to the suppressed weapon. They thudded into the bulletproof vest, ripping the material but not going any further. As the shots were fired, the two of them fell straight into the cockpit and onto the body of the hijacker. The three of them smashed against the instrument panel, and Ben heard the crunch of broken glass as they did so. The plane started screaming. Through the windscreen of the cockpit, Ben could see the sickening sight of the sea, far below but approaching at a forty-five degree angle.

They were going down.

'I've got him!' Angelo yelled, his voice thick with panic. 'Get the controls, Ben. *Get the controls!*'

Ben looked around him. There was someone else in the cockpit and in the confusion he realized it was Danny. The man was helping Angelo restrain the hijacker, whose arms were flailing and who was shouting out in a foreign language Ben didn't recognize. Just to his right was the control stick, vibrating and juddering. It took all Ben's strength to fight against the G-force of the plane, but he just managed to get his fingertips round the stick and push himself into the pilot's seat. With all his might he pulled on the control stick, straining his muscles against the force that was urging the plane downwards.

Behind him, shrieks of terror came from the cabin. '*The controls, Ben!*' Danny was still shouting. '*Get them!*'

'I'm trying, all right!' Ben yelled back, but he wasn't sure if anyone would have heard him over the ear-splitting sound of the engines. He gritted his teeth and pulled the control stick as hard as he could. '*I'm . . . try-ing . . .*' he roared.

And gradually, almost imperceptibly, the plane started to straighten.

Sweat was dripping down Ben's face as the horizon line started to level. Beside him there was scuffling and he glanced over momentarily to see the hijacker on the floor. He was a small man, but stocky, and with an angry red scar down one side of his face. His eyes were filled with fury. Danny had taken the man's gun and was holding it over him while Angelo got to his feet.

Ben snapped his attention back to the plane. He scanned the instrument panel and it was only then, to his horror, that he saw the full extent of the damage they had inflicted as they fell upon it. Half the instruments were smashed in, the dials broken. And even if the control panel had been in perfect working order, Ben realized that this was going to be a lot more difficult than flying a microlight. This was a whole different kettle of fish.

'Are you OK, Ben?'

It was Danny who was speaking. From the corner of his eye, Ben saw the hijacker being removed from the cockpit by a couple of other passengers.

'Er, kind of,' Ben answered. 'Look, I don't really know what I'm doing here. I need to try and get the radio working. I need to try and—'

As he was speaking, something flashed across the front of the plane. A deafening roar filled his ears.

'*What was that?*' he shouted.

'I don't know,' Danny replied. 'It looked like a—'

This time it was Danny's turn to be interrupted. The roar filled their ears again, and the cockpit was momentarily cast into shadow as another object shot past their field of vision.

It was only then that the radio sprang into life.

'Flight GXR1689, this is the Department of Homeland Security. Pilot, identify yourself. I repeat, pilot identify yourself. Two F-35 Lightning IIs have entered your airspace with instructions to destroy your aircraft if you do not identify yourself. I repeat, you will be taken out in the next thirty seconds if you do not identify yourself.'

Ben stared at the radio in frozen horror.

'Answer it, Ben!' Angelo shouted, and that was all it

took to snap Ben out of it. He grabbed the radio hand-set and started to yell a response.

'*Don't fire!*' he shouted. '*Don't fire! We've been hijacked but we've taken back the plane. The pilots are dead. You've got to help me land this thing!*'

But even as he spoke, Ben's eyes widened in horror. From either side of the cockpit window he could see the noses of the two F-35s. They were unbelievably close – close enough for Ben to see the pilots with their sun-glasses and military helmets – and they really didn't look like they were going away.

Chapter Six

'Pilot, identify yourself.'

The voice at the other end sounded completely unmoved by Ben's outburst.

'My name's Ben Tracey,' he screamed. 'I'm a passenger on the plane. At least I was until about a minute ago. You've got to believe me – I'm not a hijacker. Please! Tell them to pull away! They're too close – I don't know if I can keep this thing straight! If they don't, we could *all* be history!'

Radio silence. The fighter planes didn't move from their positions.

'We've taken control of the plane!' he screamed. 'They don't need to be there!'

Still silence.

'Listen to me! I'm not a hijacker! I'm just trying to keep this plane in the air, OK?' Terror exploded from his voice.

And then, suddenly, as suddenly as they had arrived, the fighter planes curved off and disappeared. Ben felt a moment of relief, but it didn't last long because the radio suddenly crackled into life again. 'Flight GXR1689, this is Miami International, do you read me?'

The voice sounded urgent.

'Yeah,' Ben replied through gritted teeth. 'I read you. Where have those two planes gone?'

'Back to base. There's nothing they can do to help you now.'

'Right. Well, thanks for getting them off my back.' *Like they were there to help me in the first place*, he thought to himself.

'Nothing to do with me, son. You must have been pretty convincing. How are you guys doing up there?'

'Oh,' Ben replied edgily, 'you know. Probably could be better.'

'How much experience you had flying a plane, son?'

Ben took a deep breath. 'Just a microlight,' he replied. 'Oh, and a few goes on a computer flight simulator.'

There was an ominous pause. 'That's it?' the voice asked.

''Fraid so.'

'And there's no one else on board with any flying experience?'

'Not as far as I know. I'm afraid you're stuck with me. Sorry.'

Another pause. 'What's your name?'

'Ben.'

'OK, Ben. Everything's going to be all right and you're going to do just fine as long as you follow my instructions carefully. Do you think you can do that?'

'Why don't we just get on with it?' Ben replied impatiently.

'Good idea, Ben. Now listen to me. You know about the hurricane?'

'I think someone might have mentioned it, yeah.'

'You need to stay calm, Ben. I don't want you to panic, but when your plane lost control just now, you changed direction. You're heading straight towards it. You've lost a lot of altitude, so you're going to start experiencing the headwinds very soon. You need to turn the plane back on course. Do you copy?'

Ben realized he was breathing heavily. His stomach had twisted into a knot at what he heard. 'Yeah, I copy. What do I need to do?'

'Can you see the instruments in front of you?' the voice asked.

'Some of them,' Ben replied. 'A lot got damaged when we attacked the hijacker.'

'Is there anything that looks like a compass?'

Ben quickly scanned the instruments in front of him. 'Nothing,' he replied curtly.

'OK,' the voice replied. 'You need to pan to the east. That'll take you out of the way. You're currently heading—'

There was a sudden burst of white noise. Ben blinked. The radio was crackling and whatever the guy at the other end was trying to tell him was lost in the interference.

'Hello!' Ben shouted. '*Hello! Do you copy?*'

But there was nothing other than an ugly-sounding hiss.

It was at precisely that moment that the winds started to hit. The whole plane shuddered with a level of turbulence Ben had never felt before. Vaguely, in the background, he heard people in the cabin shouting, but he tried to put that from his mind as he felt himself juddering in his seat. He gripped the control stick firmly and shouted into the radio. 'Do you read me? *Do you read me? I need to know which way to turn!*'

There was no reply.

The shaking was getting worse now. Ben knew he had to steer the plane away, but he couldn't tell which direction he needed to go in. A mistake now and it could be an end to everything.

'What's going on?' a voice yelled behind him.

Ben realized it was Angelo, but there was no time to

reply. 'Hold on!' he shouted. He felt all his muscles clenching as he started to pull the aircraft into a turn.

They were at an angle now, and the plane was juddering worse than ever. From the corner of his eye, Ben realized that Angelo had been thrown to the floor. There was nothing he could do about it though. He just had to hold his nerve – and the control stick. As the plane was at an angle, he saw the ocean down below from the side of the cockpit window. It made his blood freeze, made him feel like he had left his stomach a mile back. Without any instruments in front of him, he could only guess how long he should keep this turning circle going, so after a few moments, he straightened up, fervently hoping that he had redirected the plane to safety. Safety of a kind at least.

The winds were still buffeting the aircraft, however. Angelo shouted something behind him, but Ben didn't even hear what it was. All his concentration was taken up now by flying the plane, and by wondering if he had made the correct manoeuvre. It still felt like they were being flung around in the air. Maybe they were still heading straight for the hurricane. Maybe he should turn the plane round again. As that thought crossed his mind, though, he nodded his head to himself. If he kept turning, he'd get nowhere: he'd just have to trust his first instinct. He'd just have to keep to his current direction.

Danny staggered into the cockpit, doing his best to stay upright despite the shaking of the plane. 'We've tied the hijacker up,' he announced. 'What's going on in here?'

'Radio's down,' Ben said tersely. 'Something to do with the weather, I suppose. I'm trying to avoid the hurricane.'

'Er, Ben,' Angelo butted in. 'I don't want to interfere or anything, but it still feels quite windy out there.'

As if to underline Angelo's sarcastic comment, the turbulence suddenly increased dramatically. Ben grabbed the radio once more and started shouting into it again, but there was still no reply. 'What are we going to do?' Angelo demanded hysterically.

'I don't know,' Ben replied. 'Hope I'm doing the right thing, I guess.'

As he spoke, however, the turbulence subsided. Ben breathed out deeply. 'Nice one,' he heard Danny say from behind him.

'How's everyone doing back there?' he asked.

'*Non bene*,' Angelo replied weakly. 'A few people have been knocked about a bit, but they're panicking more than anything.'

'I don't blame them,' Ben muttered. He peered through the windscreen. 'Look out there,' he said quickly. 'Does that look to you like land up ahead?'

Danny and Angelo squinted into the distance. 'I

think you're right,' Angelo murmured. He turned to look at Ben. 'Do you know how to land this thing?'

Ben didn't reply. He didn't have time, because at that very moment there was another lurch as the plane seemed to dip sharply to one side. A feeling of dread crept over Ben's body as he compensated for the sudden change by steering in the opposite direction. The plane straightened up, but the change in lift was noticeable at the controls. He cursed under his breath. 'Feels like we lost an engine,' he said grimly.

Angelo stared at him, then rushed out to the cabin. When he returned, he was out of breath. 'The propellers are still turning on the bad side,' he said.

'They would do,' Ben replied. 'It's the movement of the plane that's making them go round, though, not the engine.' He furrowed his brow and stared straight ahead. 'We've got to land this thing,' he said. 'Make sure everyone's sitting down and strapped in. This isn't going to be fun.'

'You need any help here?' Danny asked.

Ben shook his head. 'Not unless you know how to land a plane,' he said.

'Well, I think you could use the company.' Danny sat in the co-pilot's seat and buckled himself in. 'If we don't get through this, Ben, I want you to know that you've been incredibly brave.'

That *wasn't* what Ben wanted to hear.

'We're going to get through it,' he said between gritted teeth.

'Yes,' said Danny. 'Yes, we are.'

They fell into an uneasy silence. Ben concentrated on keeping the aircraft straight with only the horizon line to help him. The land that they had spotted was approaching surprisingly quickly. Gradually, gently, he started to reduce the velocity and altitude. He felt sick with fear at the thought of trying to land this thing, but he knew he had no other choice but to try.

As the plane lost height, Ben noticed something. Up ahead and to one side, the sky was darkening. He felt his lips go dry – it didn't look dissimilar to the bubbling sky he had witnessed just the previous night at Alec's house. It was the storm they were escaping. It had to be.

'You'd better hold on,' Ben murmured to Danny. 'This is going to be nasty.'

The closer they got to land, the bumpier the ride became. Ben gripped the control stick fiercely, gradually reducing the altitude. From time to time he tried to kick the radio into life, but it was completely dead and in the end he just gave up and concentrated on the matter in hand: getting to land.

They were perhaps still a mile out to sea when a cloud bank seemed to come from nowhere. As he stared at it in horror, Ben heard Alec's voice in his head. *Amazing thing, nature. Always got a surprise up its sleeve.*

'You can say that again,' Ben murmured.

'What?' Danny asked.

'Nothing,' Ben replied as the plane was suddenly plunged into the cloud. Instantly he lost all visual contact with the horizon and, not having any instruments to tell him if he was level or not, he found himself flying blind, without even a few metres' visibility.

'Hold it steady, Ben,' he told himself. 'Just hold it steady.'

His breath came in deep, long lungfuls. The turbulence increased in the cloud, making it even harder to keep the plane straight, if indeed it *was* straight. It was horrible, flying without any sense of what was in front of him. Ben half expected to crash into some unseen obstacle at any moment. When finally he came below the cloud line, he realized he was at an angle and veering away from land. He straightened up and tried not to think too much about what was about to happen.

It was raining now and the sky above them was black. The winds had increased again – Ben could feel them knocking the plane around. It was worse now that he had reduced his speed. More and more he felt like a speck of dust at the mercy of some incredibly powerful forces. The sea below them was grey and rough, and it was a relief when they finally flew over land. As the plane continued to lose altitude, Ben felt a momentary flash of relief that the land ahead appeared to be un-populated. He shuddered to think what sort of devastation he would cause if he crash-landed in the middle of an urban sprawl. But as soon as that thought flew through his mind, it disappeared. He had other things to worry about, after all . . . Hurtling onwards through the sheeting rain, Ben thought he could see greenery down below. And then, a long way in the distance, he thought he could make out a long, straight road running at right angles to the direction of the plane.

'We need to try and land there,' he barked at Danny – quite why, he wasn't sure, as nobody else was helping him fly this thing. He yanked the control stick to the left. The plane veered in that direction, shuddering as it did so. Ben prayed that there wouldn't be much traffic on the road. Surely people would be taking cover from the elements, he prayed. A hurricane was hitting the mainland of Florida – he hoped most people would think it wasn't a very good time to go out for a drive.

He straightened up. They couldn't be more than a hundred metres from the ground, but now that he had a closer point of reference, Ben realized just how much the plane was shaking. The road ahead did indeed seem empty. On either side of it was what looked like swamp land and with each passing second it looked more and more likely that that was where they were going to land. Ben struggled to keep the line of the road in the middle of his sight – a task made doubly difficult by the winds and the fact that one engine was down. He was holding his breath and his muscles were burning from the strain of keeping the plane straight.

They couldn't have been more than seventy-five metres up now, but as Ben fixed his eyes on the ground ahead, one thing became perfectly clear to him.

They were going too fast.

Much too fast.

Danny must have realized it too. 'This isn't going to work, is it, Ben?' he asked, his voice strangely expressionless.

Ben glanced momentarily towards him. Danny was looking straight ahead. His face was calm. He looked like he was preparing himself for something.

Preparing himself for the end.

Ben snapped his gaze back to the landing strip. Danny was right. It wasn't going to work. He took another deep breath and prepared for the plane to hit the ground.

Miami International Airport had been all but evacuated.

At the control tower, the last remaining airport employees crowded round the bank of air-traffic control screens. Half an hour ago these screens had been illuminated with the flight information of the many aircraft in the area. Now those aircraft had been redirected north, away from the freak hurricane that was about to make landfall, and the screens were blank.

Blank, that is, except for a single plane.

They had lost radio contact some minutes ago and though they kept trying to re-establish it, it was quite clear that they weren't going to succeed. The sensible thing for them to do now was to leave the exposed environment of the control tower and find some sort of shelter from the hurricane. But while none of them said it out loud, they all felt that to do so would somehow be to abandon that doomed flight and its passengers. It was the least they could do to see it through to the end.

Jack Simpson simply couldn't take his eyes off the screen. Like all of them, he had heard the terrified voice of the kid who had taken control of the aircraft. Terrified but somehow brave – Jack wondered if he would have had the same kind of guts in that situation. He suspected not. Now, however, all they could do was watch and wait. If the plane continued on its current course, it would crash-land somewhere in the Everglades National Park, an unpopulated area that was no doubt deserted by now because of the evacuation.

But the Everglades was also where the hurricane was heading. They might be feeling the edges of it here in

Miami – and heaven knows that was bad enough – but the plane was much nearer the centre. Those passengers were going to be lucky to be alive even if they survived the impact.

Under ordinary circumstances, a whole fleet of rescue aircraft would be on standby to rush to the crash site. But these circumstances were far from ordinary. There was no way any aircraft – choppers or planes – would be able to risk flying in those circumstances. If they did, they would surely end up in the same state as the passengers on flight GXR1689.

They would end up dead.

And so there was nothing to do but leave the aircraft to its fate. Jack wanted to howl in frustration at his powerlessness. He wanted to shake his bosses and the military commanders who had decided not to engage their troops in a dangerous search and rescue mission. It was the twenty-first century, he wanted to shout. Surely something could be done.

Deep down, however, he knew that nothing could be. He knew that sometimes men simply couldn't battle against the extremes of nature. In a fight like that, there would only be one winner.

No. They would all have to wait until the hurricane passed. The storm that had just hit land was worse than anything anybody had seen in their lifetime. There would be casualties and devastation all around the southern tip of Florida. It would be shown on TV for weeks, even months afterwards. But none of it, Jack knew, would touch him as deeply as the scene that he knew was going to happen. None of it would be as bad as the pictures of a shattered plane and the burned, dismembered corpses among its wreckage. Because somewhere deep within him, Jack felt that he should have been able to do something. He should have been more in control. He should have been able to help.

Everyone in the control room gasped, Jack included. He felt his skin tingle and go cold as he blinked at the screen. The plane had disappeared, and they all knew what that meant.

Impact.

There was an instant of stunned silence. And then Jack's boss shattered the nightmare moment. 'OK, guys,' he shouted. 'Show's over. There was nothing more any of you could have done. Your priority's to get out of here and to a place of shelter. There's a bus waiting to take you off the airport grounds. Get a move on! *Go!*'

Everyone scrambled for the door. Everyone, that is, except Jack. He found himself rooted to the spot, staring at the blank screen.

His boss came up beside him. 'You couldn't have done anything, Jack,' he said quietly. 'No one could have predicted what just happened. This isn't down to you.'

Jack took a deep breath. He knew that what his boss was saying was right, but somehow that didn't make him feel much better.

It was with a heavy heart that he turned his back on the screen, left the control tower and prepared to face the storm himself.

Chapter Seven

The plane wobbled dramatically. It felt like a futile gesture, but Ben tugged at the control stick to get them straight.

Fifty metres up. The road appeared in the middle of his sights, but it was touch and go.

Twenty-five metres. The plane was speeding. *Too fast. Far too fast.*

'Hold on!' Ben shouted. They were about to hit the ground. '*HOLD ON!*'

It was only as they touched down that Ben realized he hadn't put the landing wheels down – not that he'd have known how to do it even if he'd remembered. The fuselage crunched horribly against the ground. The noise was deafening, and Ben felt a vicious shock as his body jolted fiercely. The plane bounded into the air, spinning 180 degrees as it did so before coming to land again. Ben's hands flew away from the control stick; everything in front of him became nothing but an awful, dizzy blur. It was out of his control now.

This is it, he thought to himself. *We can't possibly survive a crash like this.*

As that thought ran through his mind, the plane bounced again. Something flew up to the windscreen: it cracked and shattered. Suddenly the noise doubled before the plane bounced a third time. It was still spinning – any second now, Ben thought, and they would be plunged into the marshland on either side of the road. He closed his eyes, bent over, braced his head in his arms and prepared himself for the worst.

The noise continued to thunder in his ears.

They were going to die. There was no way they could survive this. They'd be crushed or drowned, or both. It was going to happen.

Any moment now. It was going to happen . . .

But it didn't.

It took a full minute for the aircraft to come to a halt, a full minute for the roaring of the crash landing to stop, replaced by the sound of the high winds howling through the shattered screen. Ben was shaking with fear, his breath coming in short, sharp, desperate bursts. When he dared gradually to look up, his whole body aching from the impact, he couldn't quite believe that he was still alive.

He stayed perfectly still, dumbfounded.

'You OK, Ben?' a voice croaked from beside him.

Ben looked over. Danny's face was drawn and shocked. His nose was bleeding and there was a nasty-looking cut on his forehead. But he looked like he was in one piece. 'Yeah,' Ben replied. 'I think so.' He allowed himself a rueful smile. 'Just as long as they don't make me pay for the damage.'

'I think they're more likely to give you a medal, Ben,' Danny said quietly. 'I don't know how you managed that.'

Me neither, Ben thought to himself. But for the moment he was happy to accept the praise. 'We should go and see how the others are,' he said. 'I reckon everyone was bumped around pretty hard back there – could be some casualties.'

Danny nodded and they both started to unbuckle themselves. Ben had barely stood up, however, before he heard the shouting from the cabin.

'I can smell burning!' someone yelled. 'Quickly! Something's on fire! We have to get off the plane before it blows!'

It was the sparks that had caused it. As the plane had bounced and scraped along the ground, showers of them had erupted on the undercarriage. The final bounce had ripped the metal of the fuselage and as the plane came to a halt, the sparks had showered into the hold. It hadn't taken long for the pallets of luggage to ignite, and only moments later, the whole area was billowing with smoke.

The temperature was rising rapidly. They had very little time before the fuel stores would explode . . .

The scene in the cabin was now one of utter devastation.

Oxygen masks hung from the ceiling; the overhead luggage compartments were open and their contents spilled all over the floor; several of the small oval windows were smashed in. As Ben stepped out of the cockpit, one of the cabin crew was just opening an emergency exit. The passengers crowded round, all jostling with each other to get out. Some of them were clearly injured: there were quite a few bloodied faces and a couple of the older people were limping. None of them, Ben noticed, paid him any attention, or offered any word of thanks for what he had just done. Not that he was expecting any – he was just glad to be on the ground.

Only one person approached him, and that was Angelo. His eyes were wild and he had a nasty bruise on the side of his face. Apart from that, he was remarkably unscathed.

'Where's the burning coming from?' Ben demanded immediately.

'Nobody knows,' Angelo replied.

'We need to get out quickly. If the fuel store ignites it won't matter if we're on the ground or not. This thing will go off like a firework.' Ben's voice was urgent, hurried. He looked around. 'They should open some more emergency exits, get everyone off the plane quicker.'

'They've tried,' Angelo told him. 'The opening levers were all damaged in the crash. That's the only exit that works.'

As he spoke, Ben saw an inflatable ramp being extended down to the ground. The cabin crew were doing their best to stay calm themselves, but any chance they had of keeping the other passengers composed was long gone. They were hurling themselves out of the plane, scrambling for the exit and shouting at each other. It wasn't a pretty sight. But it did appear that – against all odds – there had been no deaths or serious injuries. Everyone was getting out. The only casualties were those who had been shot: the two pilots and Brad.

Ben sniffed. The burning smell was definitely getting stronger. There were only about ten passengers plus the cabin crew left on the plane now, so he, Angelo and Danny moved down to the exit as smoke began to billow up into the passenger area. The cabin crew were on the inflatable ramp as they approached and they threw themselves down as the trio prepared to exit.

The wind outside was screaming now, and Ben felt the force of it against his body even inside the plane. He was just about to slide down the ramp when he remembered something. 'The hijacker!' he barked over the noise. 'Where is he?'

Danny pointed further down the plane. 'Back there,' he shouted. 'Tied to one of the cabin crew's seats.'

Ben looked at him in amazement. 'We can't just leave him there. We've got to get him off.'

'But—' Angelo stuttered. 'But, Ben, he was trying to kill us all.'

Ben stood up. 'I don't care.' He was having to yell above the noise of the wind and a sudden gust that came in through the exit nearly knocked him down. 'If we leave him to die in here,' he yelled, 'we're as bad as he is!'

With that, he ran down the aisle of the plane. 'Ben!' Angelo shouted after him, but he ignored his friend.

The hijacker was just where Danny had said he would be. His seat faced the back of the plane and someone had found a length of rope – enough to tie him very securely. The knots looked big and fiendish, and they kept him firmly in place. The result was that, unlike many of the passengers, he had come through the crash-landing with barely a mark to his body.

It was the first time Ben had had a proper look at the

guy, and though he didn't exactly spend a lot of time gazing at his features, he felt as if the hijacker's face would be burned on his memory for the rest of his life. He was a small man, but well built with dark skin and short black hair. Along the left-hand side of his face was a pale scar. But what Ben noticed more than anything else was the look in his eyes. It was a strange mixture of hate and passion. Certainly the man didn't look scared. He held his head up proudly.

Ben didn't say anything to him. He couldn't think of anything *to* say. Instead, he approached and started trying to untie one of the knots.

His panicked fingers couldn't move fast enough. He picked at the thick rope, a freezing fear passing through his body at the thought that the plane could explode any second. Whoever had tied these knots, however, had known what they were doing. No matter how hard he worked at them, he couldn't even loosen the things. The hijacker remained perfectly still. He stared straight at Ben – an uncomfortable sensation – the look of loathing etched on his face.

'You could at least help me,' Ben hissed urgently as he continued trying to untie the knots. But the hijacker didn't reply. He just sat there, as if waiting for the inevitable, the smoke gradually obscuring his features.

'*We've got to get off the plane!*' Angelo's urgent voice

came from nowhere. Ben spun round to see him standing nearby.

'I thought you'd already gone,' Ben observed curtly.

'Ben, *please*. It's not safe.'

Ben ignored him and continued trying to undo the ropes. With an impatient sigh, Angelo joined him, both of them crowding round the hijacker as they desperately tried to release him. The arrival of Angelo, however, seemed to have an effect on the tightly bound man. He started to mumble something in a foreign language. Ben didn't understand what he was saying, but he certainly got the gist of it: they were words of absolute hate. The two of them did their best to ignore him.

Above the noise of the wind, Ben and Angelo heard Danny's voice. 'We have to get off now!' he called. 'The burning's getting worse. It could go up any moment!' Ben's fingers were bleeding from the roughness of the rope, but none of the knots had even budged. He felt Angelo grab him by the arms.

'Ben,' the Italian said firmly. 'We can't undo him. We've *got* to get off this plane. There's no point all of us dying.'

Ben felt the frustration boiling up in him, but he knew Angelo was right. He looked at the hijacker. 'I tried,' he said quietly.

It was only then that the hijacker spoke in English.

'You think you have beaten me,' he hissed. 'But you haven't. I welcome death, but the arm of my people is longer than you think.' He looked at Angelo. 'You will pay for what you have done,' he spat. 'Believe me, you will pay.'

'I haven't done anything,' Angelo replied. He turned to Ben. 'Come on,' he said. 'Let's get out of here.'

Ben nodded, and without another look at the hijacker, he crawled back up the aisle – following the emergency lights in the floor – with Angelo to the exit.

Danny had left the aircraft just before them and was waiting for them at the bottom of the inflatable ramp. None of the other passengers were in view. His hair was blowing in the heavy wind and he was screaming up at them, although they couldn't hear a word he was saying above the howling gale.

'*Jump!*' Angelo yelled, and together they slid down the ramp and onto the ground below.

The moment he hit firm ground, Ben took in his surroundings. The plane had come to a halt at right angles to the road and it was only then that he realized how lucky they had been. It was not a wide road – indeed it was more of a mud track – and on either side of it was marshland that seemed to stretch as far as they could see. The wind was whipping the water on either side of them into a dangerous-looking frenzy, and the reeds and other vegetation were being blown all over the place. The air was thick with flying plant debris; the sky was dark and angry.

Almost as though they were one person, Ben, Angelo and Danny ran away from the plane along the road. They were a good thirty metres away when Ben suddenly stopped. 'The others!' he shouted above the sound of the wind. 'Where are they?'

The three of them looked all around.

'The cabin crew must have taken them round the other side of the plane,' Angelo shouted.

'We should try and stick together,' said Ben. 'If any-one sends out a search and rescue party, it'd be much better if we were all in one group.'

It was Danny who stopped him. 'I don't think it's a good idea to go past the plane again,' he shouted. Ben and Angelo turned to look at him. 'Look, Ben,' he continued, 'I'm not saying you did the wrong thing stopping to try and free the hijacker, but we lost a lot of time back there. If something's burning, we'd be idiots to approach the plane again. We need to stay well away, even if it means splitting up from the others.'

Ben hesitated. He knew that what Danny was saying made sense, but at the same time he didn't like losing the safety they would have in numbers.

Suddenly, however, the decision was made for him.

There were two explosions. The first made more

noise than anything else – a great thunderclap that shook Ben's body to its very core.

'*Run!*' he yelled.

It was the second explosion that threw them all to the earth. They had started sprinting away from the plane when it happened, and as the force of it hurled them through the air and onto the ground, they all instinctively covered their heads with their arms. The first thing they felt was the heat. With all the energy of a thousand ovens, it felt for a few grisly seconds as if it was scorching the skin from their bodies. Ben heard Angelo yelling in terror before he started to feel bits of debris raining down on them. He didn't dare look up in case something hit him in the eye, but he knew they had to get out of range of the debris as quickly as possible to avoid being injured.

Danny had obviously had the same thought. '*Get up!*' he yelled. '*We need to keep running!*'

Ben and Angelo didn't have to be told twice. They pushed themselves to their feet and started sprinting away from the horrific, burning fireball that had exploded only metres behind them.

Chapter Eight

They ran and they ran.

None of them looked behind them. They didn't need to – it was clear that the explosion had been massive. The heat was still fierce and the debris, blown high in the air, was now falling randomly to the ground, scattered all over the place by the high winds. Ben stumbled and almost fell; as he did so, he felt Danny's strong hand grip his arm and pull him up. They carried on running.

They only stopped when they seemed to be out of range of the debris. Gasping for breath, they turned round and finally looked back. The plane was a blazing inferno. Now it was alight, it seemed much bigger than it had done before. Chunks of burning metal were strewn all over the path, mini bonfires that occasionally popped and exploded dangerously. The high winds made the flames dance and Ben saw – with alarm – that the dry grass on the road that they were following was catching fire, which was slowly approaching them.

He spun round in the opposite direction. The road trailed off into the distance. It was too murky to see where it led.

It was Angelo who spoke first. 'We need to let some-one know we're here,' he said. Pulling out his mobile phone, he looked at the screen.

'Anything?' Ben asked.

The Italian shook his head. 'Nothing. It must be the storms.' He looked around. 'Where are we?' he asked.

Ben had been thinking the same thing, and he reckoned he had an answer. 'I think it must be the Everglades,' he called above the wind.

Angelo's brow furrowed. 'I've never been here before . . .' he said uncertainly. 'I've heard people talk-ing about it, of course . . .'

'It's a national park,' Ben said. He couldn't quite remember where he'd learned this stuff. 'Marshlands, mangrove swamps, cypress glades – that kind of thing.' He looked around. 'Goes on for miles.'

'Great,' Angelo murmured. 'How do we get out?'

There was pause. Danny spoke next. He pointed across the marshland to his right. 'The plane came from that direction,' he shouted. 'So that must be south. That means the track we're on must go from east to west.'

Ben cursed. 'We need to head east,' he said. 'That's the way out of the park but . . .' His voice trailed off. There was no way they were going to get past the burning plane. To make matters worse, the dry grass had continued to catch alight and with the aid of the winds the flames were coming closer and closer. 'We haven't got a choice,' he shouted. 'We need to head west.' He pointed out to the swamps. 'Unless anyone fancies a swim.'

'In that?' Angelo pointed to the tempestuous waters. 'No thanks.'

Danny looked west. 'So are we agreed, then?' he asked. 'We keep going that way.'

Ben and Angelo nodded and the three hurried off again.

They half walked, half ran. It was difficult to move. The gusts of wind were unpredictable and things were flying in the air. None of them could tell what the debris was, or where it came from, but more than once Ben had to cover his head suddenly to protect himself from some unknown flying object. Now and then he would stop to look behind them: the plane was still burning fiercely and no matter how much distance they put between them and the blazing aircraft, it still seemed to light up the whole sky.

The wind was whipping itself up into even more of a frenzy now. It felt like the hurricane was getting stronger and closer. 'We need shelter!' Ben shouted as they hurried grimly on. As he spoke, a gust of wind caught the water of the marshland near him and a wave of muddy water splashed over the grassy road, soaking the three of them and knocking Angelo to the ground. Ben and Danny helped him up, and together they carried on going.

They had been heading west for perhaps fifteen minutes when they noticed the road becoming wider. Up ahead, through the gloom, Ben thought he saw a building of some description. They hurried towards it.

It was a single-storey structure with a pitched roof. Several of the roof slates had been blown away and had smashed on the ground, but otherwise the building was intact. A big sign had been uprooted and was lying on the road. Ben approached it and read what it said. 'EVERGLADES NATIONAL PARK' it announced in big letters. 'WARDENS' STATION AND INFORMATION CENTER'.

'Let's get in out of the wind!' Ben shouted. Together they approached the building.

The main door was open and banging to and fro in the wind. Ben grabbed the edge of it and held it fast while the other two hurried inside. He then pulled it shut. The latch clicked, but he didn't know how long it would hold.

They found themselves in a single big room. It was

completely deserted and it showed signs of having been evacuated quickly. A postcard stand had been knocked over and nobody had bothered to pick it up; a couple of rucksacks were abandoned on the floor. Towards the back of the room there was a long counter with information leaflets stacked up upon it. On two sides of the room there were long, low windows looking out onto the marshland; the remainder of the walls themselves were covered with posters of the various parts of the Everglades. Ben saw images of marshland, thick cypress groves, vast pools and rivers. Under any other circumstances they would have been fascinating and he'd have been chomping at the bit to go and explore the region. Not today, though. Today, this vast natural park felt like the last place on earth he wanted to be.

He felt like they were the last *people* on earth too. There was something unbelievably spooky about being alone in a place that had been deserted, and for a while the three of them remained silent, looking around and taking in their new surroundings. The wind was still howling outside, but now they had a bit of shelter it seemed a lot quieter.

Ben realized he was shivering. His clothes were soaking wet and the wind had blown them cold. 'We should try and find something dry to put on,' he announced as he started rummaging through the rucksacks that had been left on the ground. All he found, however, were some thin waterproof coats. 'I guess we might need these,' he murmured as he handed them round and tried to forget about the way his jeans were clinging clammily to his skin. The other two looked uncomfortable as well. Angelo's long hair was strewn all over his frightened face, and Danny's slicked-back hair was a mess. They, too, shivered with the cold.

'Look over here,' Angelo said. He was looking at something on one of the walls. Ben and Danny approached and they saw what it was: a map of the park. Towards the bottom of it there was a yellow arrow marked with the words 'YOU ARE HERE'.

Ben studied the map. The road they were on led to the eastern edge of the park, but to go that way they would have to pass the burning debris of the plane. As the road carried on west, it just seemed to peter out into the marshland. It looked to Ben very much like they were stranded.

It was as they were staring at the map that a sudden gust of wind shrieked overhead. There was a loud crash as one of the wide windows dramatically shattered. Shards of glass crashed over the inside of the room like a shower of diamonds; the three of them pressed against the opposite wall, thankful that they weren't in range of the exploding window.

'It's not safe here,' Ben muttered.

'I don't see that we have much option,' Danny

told him. 'It looks like we're cut off on both sides.'

An ominous silence fell over their little group. Ben edged away from the map and looked at another poster. 'WILDLIFE OF THE EVERGLADES' it read in big, sunny letters across the top; below, there were pictures of different animals. Ben's eyes fell upon the image of an alligator. He read the words under the image of that ugly-looking beast. '*Gators are everywhere in the Everglades*,' it read. '*If you see one, keep your distance. You never know if it's had its lunch yet!*'

Under the picture of the alligator was what looked like a big cat. Its fur was a light brown colour, it had sharp, pointed ears and a ferocious look in its eyes. Ben read what the poster had to say about it. '*The Florida Panther is a critically endangered species. There are only thought to be between 80 and 100 panthers left in this part of the world and they avoid humans, so if you see one, you're incredibly lucky.*' The panther seemed to stare out of the picture at Ben, who wasn't sure quite how lucky he would feel if he came face to face with one of the animals.

His eyes only skirted over the third picture. Ever since his trip to the Congo, Ben had had a thing about snakes, and the snake that was depicted here was a big one. '*The Burmese Python*,' the text underneath it explained, '*is not native to the United States. Many people, however, keep them as pets. Unfortunately, when they grow too big to be manageable, these snakes are let out into the wild. The Everglades provides a perfect breeding environment for them, and they have thrived and multiplied here. Burmese Pythons can grow up to seven metres long. Even when they are smaller than this, they are perfectly capable of overpowering and killing a fully grown adult!'*

Ben shuddered slightly. The very thought of it made him feel a bit faint. He sensed Danny stepping up to him. 'Bit of a day,' his companion observed.

'Yeah,' Ben said. 'You could say that.'

'You did an amazing thing in that plane, Ben. If it wasn't for you, everyone would have been killed.'

Ben shrugged. 'Just fluke,' he said. 'That hijacker was pretty determined.'

At the thought of the hijacker, something crossed Ben's mind. Since they had escaped the plane, everything had happened so quickly – too quickly, certainly, for him to think too deeply about the events of the last few hours. But as he stood there, he remembered what the hijacker had said before they left the plane. *You think you have beaten me, but you haven't.*

He looked over at Angelo, who was sitting on the floor now, hugging his legs. 'Angelo,' he said sharply. 'What do think he meant?'

Angelo looked at him quizzically. '*Cosa?*'

'The hijacker. All that stuff about not having beaten him.'

His Italian friend looked thoughtful. 'I don't know,' he mused. 'Maybe—' His eyes widened. 'Maybe there's another plane. Another attack.'

Ben thought about that for a moment. 'I don't think so,' he said. 'Don't forget, there was a special reason for him targeting that plane.' He didn't say any more – Angelo had begged him not to reveal to anyone that his dad was the owner of the oil refinery, and he wasn't about to betray that confidence even in front of Danny. 'Do you remember what Brad said, before he—' Ben hesitated. 'Before he died,' he said finally. 'You know, about hijackers working in groups and how it was weird there was just one of them.'

Angelo looked at him sharply, and so did Danny. 'What do you mean?' the man said.

Ben took a deep breath as all sorts of thoughts whizzed round his brain. 'Think about it,' he said. 'If you were trying to hijack a plane, would you do it alone?'

A look of confusion crossed Danny's face. 'Probably not,' he said. 'But if there was someone else, why didn't they do something to help him when it all started to go wrong?'

'What could they have done?' Angelo butted in. 'They'd have had to take on all of us.'

They fell silent for a moment as the implication of what they had just said hit them. 'The others,' Ben said

103

a bit breathlessly. 'They could still have one of the hijackers among them. Who knows what they're going to try and do – the other passengers could be in a lot of danger.'

CRASH! As he spoke, a second window burst in, sending all three of them crouching to the floor for cover. 'What?' Angelo shouted. 'More danger than this?'

'We've got to warn them!' Ben said, ignoring Angelo's comment. 'He could be planning anything.'

'Er, Ben,' Angelo pointed out. 'In case you hadn't noticed, there's a blazing plane wreckage between us and them, and we're in the middle of a hurricane. Haven't you saved enough lives for one day?'

But Ben wasn't listening. He pushed himself up to his feet and rushed over to the counter, his shoes crunching on shards of broken glass as he went. On the counter there were perhaps fifteen different leaflets, all of them advertising something different to do in the Everglades. Ben grabbed them all and started leafing through them. He had skim-read six or seven before he found something that captured his attention.

'Look at this,' he called to the others. He waved the leaflet in the air and hurried back to them.

On the front of the leaflet was a picture of some kind of boat. It was gaudy yellow in colour with a canopy over the top. At the back there was what looked like an enormous circular fan and at the top of the leaflet were some words: '*Airboat Tours of the Everglades.*' Ben turned the leaflet over. There was a little map. 'Look,' he said, pointing at it. 'The airboats are moored not far from here. We just need to keep heading west and we'll be able to find one and get round the plane by going on the water.'

Angelo looked at him as if he was mad. 'Ben,' he said. 'Haven't you had enough excitement for one day? Have you seen what it's like out there? If the boats aren't capsized already, they soon will be.'

'Fine, Angelo,' Ben shouted, his frustration showing in his voice. 'You stay here if you want to. I'm going to warn the others.'

Chapter Nine

The two others looked at him in silence. Angelo glanced out into the howling winds outside. 'All right, Ben,' he said finally. 'You win.'

The minute he said that, Danny was on the move. Behind the counter there was a door. Danny hurried towards it, opened it up and disappeared into the room beyond. Angelo and Ben exchanged a look, then followed.

It looked like a changing room. There were pegs on the walls and a few metal cabinets. A few items of clothing were strewn all around. 'Wardens need somewhere to change,' Danny said curtly. 'But I bet, somewhere round here—' He stood in the centre of the room looking around until his eyes fell upon the metal cabinets. Striding towards them, he tried to open one, but it was locked. He searched around again. Standing up against one corner was an umbrella, which he swiftly grabbed.

'Er, Danny,' Ben said. 'It's a hurricane. I don't think a brolly's going to be much good.'

Danny just winked at him. He forced the edge of the umbrella into the small gap between one of the cabinet doors and the frame, then yanked it sharply. The flimsy metal door buckled and swung open. Danny rummaged inside but clearly found nothing of interest, so he turned his attention to the second door. Within seconds, it too was open; but again there was nothing much inside.

The third cabinet, though, was a bit different.

The minute Danny forced the door open, a brief smile played across his lips. 'Bingo,' he muttered. He stepped forward and pulled a double-barrelled shotgun from the cabinet. 'I knew they'd have some kind of firearm hidden away,' he said. Carefully he propped the gun up against the wall, then fished around inside the cabinet before pulling out a small cardboard box. 'Ammunition,' he said shortly. 'The shotgun will only take two rounds at a time, but it should be enough to get us out of a sticky situation.' He looked meaningfully at Ben. 'Who knows what your little plan holds in store, Ben?'

Ben felt himself blushing slightly, but he did his best to ignore the comment and they all left the changing room.

Back in the main area, Danny emptied one of the abandoned rucksacks, placed the box of ammo inside and then slung it over his back. He broke the shotgun into a V shape before resting it over his shoulder. He looked, Ben thought, like he knew what he was doing. It was quite comforting.

Danny looked at the two of them. 'Ready?' he asked.

'Ready.'

'Let's go then.' He opened the main door. Instantly the howling of the wind increased in their ears, and a gust whooshed through into the room, so strong that it felt almost as if someone had hit Ben in the stomach. They pushed their way out and started forging west in the direction, they hoped, of the boats.

Even in the short time they had been inside, the sky had changed. It was darker now, and the clouds were scudding by as if someone was fast-forwarding a video. There was also a smell of burning in the air – a reminder that the blazing plane wasn't too far away, still polluting the area with its black, billowing clouds. Looking back, Ben could still see a glow in the distance. Just thinking about the plane and what had happened on it sent a shiver down his spine, so he turned his back on it and continued struggling through the wind.

The water had been choppy before, but it was much rougher now. Ben was aware of the other two eyeing it unenthusiastically as they approached the boat mooring. It was a small pier made of wood. As they got closer Ben saw that some of the slats that made up the floor of the pier had blown away in the wind. The boats themselves – there were three of them tied to the pier – were not that big. Maybe three metres in length. They were bashing against each other, knocked around by the force of the elements.

'Look!' Angelo shouted. He pointed out across the marshland.

Ben squinted his eyes. About fifty metres away there was a fourth boat. It had obviously broken away from the pier and had been hurled across the water by the hurricane. Now it was in trouble.

Big trouble.

Half of the small boat's hull was submerged. The canopy that had covered the top for shade had come loose on one corner and had filled with wind. It was billowing like a sail and pulling the boat further onto one side. The trio stood and stared at it, their hair blowing in the wind. No one said so, but Ben reckoned the other two were thinking the same as him: if anyone had been on that boat, they'd be going swimming. And a dip in those rough, muddy waters was the last thing any of them wanted in this weather.

'Maybe a bit of weight in the boat would steady it,' Angelo shouted uncertainly. The three of them edged further towards the pier. They were almost standing on it now, but neither Ben nor Danny replied to the Italian boy. Watching the boat, his suggestion seemed a bit too much to hope for. It was sinking fast. It reminded Ben of the pictures he'd seen of the *Titanic* – smaller, obviously, but going down in just the same way, and just as fast. They stared at it silently for a good two minutes, by which time the vessel was completely underwater.

The writing was on the wall. There was no way they could take to the water.

It was Angelo who said so first. 'There's no point being stupid about it, Ben. We can't help the other passengers if we're on a sinking boat.'

Ben knew he was right. 'Come on,' he said. 'Let's go back to the wardens' station. I guess we'll just have to sit out the storm.'

As one, they turned to leave. And as one, they stopped in their tracks.

Ben felt his muscles freezing.

There were five of them. Five alligators. Ben didn't know if they were fully grown adults, but from the size of them he reckoned they couldn't be far off. They had obviously approached while the three of them had been looking out across the marshland and now they were only metres away. Ben knew nothing about alligator behaviour, but you didn't need to know anything to see that they seemed agitated. Their long, scaly tails lashed out like whips and occasionally they would snap aggressively at each other.

'Where . . . where did they come from?' Angelo stammered from behind gritted teeth.

'Marshland, I guess,' Ben replied, edging nervously backwards. 'If I was one of them I wouldn't want to stay in the water when it's like this.'

A sudden movement as one of the gators shuffled forwards. It was surprisingly fast, and Ben and Angelo both stumbled as they stepped backwards onto the pier. Behind them, Ben heard the sound of Danny fumbling in his rucksack for ammunition, but before the older man could load the gun the nervous animals had grown bolder. They were crowding round the end of the pier now, snarling and snapping at each other to get onto it.

'They're hungry!' Ben shouted. His voice sounded high-pitched and nervous. 'The wind's forced them out of the water and they haven't had anything to eat!'

One of the alligators made it onto the pier; the three of them ran to the end. Danny was still fumbling with his gun, but it was clear he wasn't going to get it loaded in time.

There was only one thing they could do.

'*Jump!*' yelled Ben.

He was the first to leap into the boat that was moored at the end of the pier. He wobbled and rocked as his feet hit the hull, and he had to grab on firmly to the side of the unstable boat to stop himself from falling in.

'*Come on!*' he screamed. There were more gators on the pier, and the leader was halfway along by now. Angelo jumped; the boat rocked dangerously again. Now it was just Danny who needed to get off the pier. He threw the gun first, which clattered heavily onto the boat, followed by the rucksack full of ammo. Just as he was about to hurl himself off the pier, the lead alligator snapped at his heels.

'*Jump, Danny!*' the two of them shouted above the howling wind. '*Jump!*'

He jumped.

And as he jumped, the alligator opened its gaping mouth. It tried to grab Danny's leg but missed. Instead, its jaws clamped around the rope that was tying the boat to the pier. Furiously the alligator started to shake the rope, so when Danny landed the vessel was wobbling more unevenly than before. Instantly he lost his footing and with a shout he splashed into the water.

It all happened so quickly. Ben reached his arm out to grab Danny, who stretched to take hold of Ben's hand. But before they could make contact, the alligator's sharp teeth tore through the mooring rope. Like a pebble released from a catapult, the boat shot away from the pier, driven by the roaring wind. Ben and Angelo were away from the danger of the alligator; but Danny was still flailing in the rough water.

Ben knew he must be shouting, but he couldn't hear the man's voice above the storm.

'We've got to get him!' Angelo roared, but Ben was already on it. Still holding on firmly to the side of the dangerously swaying boat, he edged towards the back end of it. There was an intricate-looking motor there. Ben struggled to find the starting cord; when he finally did, he gave it a good yank.

Nothing but an unimpressive-sounding splutter.

He looked over his shoulder – they were moving alarmingly quickly away from where Danny was struggling in the water. From that distance they couldn't see the alligators, but they couldn't have gone far.

He pulled the starting cord again. Still nothing. Only on the third time did the motor kick into life and start turning over.

'We've got power!' Ben shouted. His voice was hoarse now from all the screaming, but he only had to yell louder now that he had to make himself heard above the growling motor as well as the wind.

Angelo didn't reply. He was too busy holding grimly onto the side of the boat, his skin a sickly shade of white. Ben clambered to the front, his body clattering uncomfortably against the hard benches in the middle of the hull as he did so. He cursed as he felt his body bruising with the impact, but finally he grabbed hold of the boat's steering wheel and knocked the throttle stick forward.

All of a sudden, the boat surged ahead. In the split second it took for a huge wave to come crashing over the boat, Ben realized he had moved far too quickly and in the wrong direction. Now his eyes were full of water, his clothes soaked. He felt the boat tip dangerously to one side before it righted itself. Looking over his shoulder, he saw that Angelo had been thrown into the centre of the boat, which had filled with a good few inches of water.

'Hold on!' he shouted. 'I'm heading for the shore.'

The second time he surged forward, he moved much more slowly. Even then it was difficult as the wind was squally and gusty. It kept coming at them from different directions, which made it incredibly hard to steer the vessel; and waves continued to splash over the side from different, unexpected directions.

They made painfully slow progress towards Danny, who kept disappearing below the random surges of the water. Ben didn't have the sensation that it was particularly deep where they were, but that didn't make it any less dangerous. For some reason he heard his mum's voice sounding in his head. '*A baby can drown in an inch of bath water, you know.*' Yeah, thought Ben grimly.

And a fully grown man can drown in the Everglade marshes in the middle of a hurricane, no problem at all.

Ben couldn't have said how long it took to get near to the spluttering Danny, but by the time they did his muscles were in agony. He could see now why the older man had stayed in the water: the alligators had left the pier and were now at the water's edge. They seemed reluctant to enter the turbulent marshes, although a couple of them seemed to be becoming braver and had started to slide their bodies closer to Danny.

When the boat was only a few metres away, Ben killed their speed. He pointed to a safety ring that was tied to the side of the boat and shouted at Angelo. 'Throw him the ring! I'll try and keep the boat steady.'

It wasn't easy. Buffeted by the wind and the waves, the boat seemed to have taken on a life of its own. Ben struggled to stop it turning of its own accord and drifting away from Danny as Angelo untied the ring.

'Quickly, Angelo,' Ben shouted. 'The alligators – they're slipping into the water.' He had just seen one of the scaly beasts disappear into the marsh despite the conditions. That must mean it was hungry enough to risk the dangers of the water in its search for food. And if it was food the gator wanted, Danny would be first choice from the menu.

Angelo stood up in the boat, steadied himself and hurled the ring overboard.

It landed close to Danny, but not quite close enough. The older man had to struggle through the water to grab it. 'Pull me in!' he shouted just as his fingers clutched the edge of the ring. There was panic in his voice. Angelo pulled, heaving on the rope like it was a tug o' war. It was obviously a struggle for him, so Ben left the steering wheel and went to help him. They stayed standing with difficulty, but gradually managed to pull him towards them.

Danny stretched out and grabbed the side of the boat. It wasn't a big vessel, and as he pulled himself up, it tilted sharply.

'*Alligator!*' Ben screamed. Only metres behind Danny he had caught a glimpse of the reptile surging through the water. He and Angelo grabbed Danny's arms and pulled him on board.

Not a moment too soon.

The alligator emerged from the water with terrifying swiftness. Its jaws snapped in the air, but they caught nothing.

Danny was on board. Soaked, breathless and white with fear. But safe.

For now, at least.

Chapter Ten

At the South Miami Oil Refinery, it was panic stations.

Nobody there knew about the plane. Nobody knew how close they had come to disaster. And nobody cared. They had other things to worry about. The hurricane was on its way, and the whole place was being shut down. All non-essential staff had already been evacuated from the premises. The final hangers-on – a few management and some security guards – would be out of there within half an hour. They all knew that an oil refinery was the last place you wanted to be in conditions like this.

In the chaos and the confusion, however, one man had managed to slip in unobserved.

He was a good-looking person, tall and with chiselled features. He hadn't shaved for a day or two, but somehow that only made him look more distinguished. More trustworthy. And he liked it that way. His black jeans fitted him well, as did his black jacket; and as he approached the oil refinery he had a small but heavy black rucksack slung over his right shoulder.

The winds were already strong here – not as strong as they were going to get, he knew, but fierce enough to make the high, wire-mesh fences that cordoned off the boundary to the refinery rattle in the breeze.

He was approaching from the south side. His car had been dumped at a nearby parking lot, and he had crossed a highway to get here. The road had been full of traffic – everyone was fleeing the area – and as he crouched by the wire fence he knew that although people *could* see him from the highway, none of them would be paying him any attention.

The fence was shaking violently. He pulled a pair of wire-cutters from his bag, then held the rattling fence in one hand and started to snip away at the mesh. It was difficult, and he was glad of the black leather gloves he was wearing. But before long he had cut a hole big enough for him to crawl through.

He skirted round the edge of the boundary towards the western entrance. There was an entry checkpoint here, but now he was inside the oil refinery's boundary fence he didn't need to be bothered by that. Hidden by a long line of low, breeze-block buildings, he walked towards the edges of the refinery itself.

It was like a small city. Huge, metallic, industrial-looking towers stretched up into the sky. Some of them had flames coming out of the top that licked into the sky; others were billowing smoke that was hardly any different to the grey clouds scudding overhead. A number of the towers had metal ladders fixed to their sides, but of course no one was using them now. Hardly anybody was on the site, in any case. There were enormous containers the size of several houses – these too had ladders on them – and everywhere there were more of the little breeze-block office buildings that he was using to hide behind. A main road led up into the centre of the refinery, and lines of lorries were parked along it in neat little groups. He supposed that ordinarily there were fewer trucks here, but no one was going to be delivering oil at the moment. Not until the storm had passed.

Just as that thought crossed his mind, there was a sudden howling of the wind. It threatened to knock him over so, quite calmly, he pressed his back against one of the breeze-block walls and waited for it to pass. Then he continued on his way.

For five minutes he headed towards the refinery. He was going to have to be careful here. He wasn't dressed for this area.

He stopped, caught his breath, and looked around.

At the base of one of the towers he saw what he

wanted: an oil-refinery worker. They were few and far between, and he knew how important it was for him not to get away. The worker wore jeans and a luminous green jacket. His head was covered by a yellow hard hat.

Quickly, the man rummaged in his rucksack before pulling something out and hiding it inside his leather jacket. Only then did he step out into the main road.

'Hey!' he called. 'You there. You heading out?' Ordinarily the man's accent was English, but for the purposes of this conversation he put on an American accent.

The worker turned to look at him. He shook his head and pointed in the air as if to say that he couldn't hear what the man was saying because of the wind.

'You heading out of the refinery?' the man repeated himself, his voice louder now. 'I could use a lift.' As he spoke he hurried across the road towards where the worker was standing.

The worker looked at him curiously as he approached, clearly surprised that someone dressed in jeans and a leather jacket should be this far into the refinery. But he seemed on edge, keen to get off the site and away to a place of relative safety – so if he was concerned about the man's presence here, he didn't say so. Instead he jerked his thumb over his shoulder. 'This way, pal,' he called. 'I'm parked up back here. You're in luck – I was just leaving.'

He turned and walked in the direction he had pointed.

Now that the worker's back was turned, the man worked quickly and deftly. The Beretta 92FS that he pulled from inside his jacket was his favourite pistol, and he would only need one of its fifteen rounds to carry out the job in hand. He swiftly raised it so that it was pointing at the back of the man's head.

And then he fired.

The shot rang out, echoing around the refinery. It was loud, but somehow it didn't seem out of place here, and he wasn't worried that anyone would come running. They would probably just think it was something to do with the wind.

The shot itself was well placed: just below the rim of the hard hat, just above the line of his luminous green jacket. The worker fell instantly to the ground. The man didn't waste any time: he dragged him out of sight of the road and quickly, before the blood could spoil his clothes, he started to undress him. Moments later he was wearing the regulation uniform of a South Miami Oil Refinery employee. He left his own clothes in a bundle by the corpse before, without a moment's remorse for what he had done, he slung his rucksack back over his shoulder and started hurrying further into the refinery.

There was a job to do.

There was money to be earned.

Everything was going according to plan. He just prayed that it would continue to do so.

Ben, Angelo and Danny gripped on tightly to the side of the boat. It was still being jostled and blown around by the wind, but for the moment they had something else to worry about. It wasn't far to the shore and in any other circumstances they'd have made straight for it. But there was no way they could do that. No way at all. Because all along the shoreline the alligators had congregated – not just the four or five that had chased them off the pier, but dozens. More than they could count.

'What are we going to do?' Angelo shouted.

Ben stared at the gators, his brow furrowed. It was dangerous in the water, but it was far more dangerous back on land. 'We haven't got any choice,' he screamed back. 'We can't get back to the shore, and we still need to warn the others. We need to try and get the boat past the plane wreckage, see what things are like back there.'

As he spoke, the three of them looked in the direction of the plane. It was out of sight, but there was still an ominous orange glow lighting up the sky from that direction. And the water looked threatening to say the least.

'OK,' Danny called. 'If we're going to do it, let's do it.' As he spoke, he secreted the shotgun and ammo in a long compartment under one of the seats. 'Do you feel like you've got the hang of this thing?'

Ben nodded.

'All right, then. You drive. Angelo and I will use our weight to try and keep the boat steady.'

Ben took his seat at the helm of the boat. As gently as possible, he turned it round. Almost immediately there was a howling gust of wind. It filled the canopy above them like a sail and suddenly they were toppling to one side. He heard Angelo screaming as the edge of the boat tipped to the water's edge; Ben himself had to clutch onto the steering wheel with all his might before Danny hurled his weight to the other side of the boat and it righted itself again.

He gritted his teeth. 'Most of the gusts are coming offshore,' he said. 'We're sailing square to the wind – that's what filling the canopy.'

'So what do we do?' Angelo demanded.

Ben could only give it a moment's thought. 'Tack in and out,' he shouted. 'That way we can keep better control of the boat.' He turned the vessel so they were pointing out to sea at an angle towards the plane.

It was tough going. Waves kept splashing over the side and the motor barely seemed powerful enough to counteract the force of the winds. The canopy above them flapped noisily. Ben was blinded by the spray; he struggled to be able to tell where he was going and more than once he found himself pointing in a completely different direction to what he thought. When he had motored out perhaps thirty metres he prepared to turn the boat and tack back in.

That was when it all went wrong.

Ben didn't know what it was that upturned the boat. A combination of things, probably: the wind, an awkward wave, the way he was turning. But suddenly he found himself under. Lungfuls of water crashed up his nose and for a moment he couldn't tell which way up he was. He kicked his legs hard and felt himself move through the water, but as he did so there was a brutal crack against his head. He only had a split second to realize that he had whacked his head against the body of the boat before he lost consciousness.

He didn't know how long he was out. It couldn't have been more than a few seconds, because next thing he knew, Angelo was dragging him to the surface. The Italian boy had his arms wrapped around Ben's torso and was grunting with exertion as their heads broke through the water. Ben coughed and spluttered – half the marsh seemed to explode from his lungs – and he only had a brief moment to see Danny standing on the upturned hull of the boat, desperately trying to right it, before they went under again.

After the noise of the wind, it was peculiarly silent underwater. Peaceful almost. As soon as they emerged again, however, the howling filled their ears. Ben was still dizzy from the bump on his head. It was disorientating. The thought of the alligators, though, soon brought him back to reality.

'It's OK,' he spluttered to Angelo. 'I can swim.'

'You sure?'

'Only one way to find out.' He struggled out of Angelo's grasp and started treading water.

Danny was about ten metres away from them. He was standing on the edge of the boat now and as Ben watched he saw the older man use his weight slowly to right the boat. It creaked upright as Danny scrambled aboard; Ben and Angelo started swimming with all their strength towards it. Ben's chest burned from the exhaustion, and it seemed to take an age before Danny's strong grasp was pulling first him and then Angelo back up onto the boat. His Italian friend fell to the floor, lying on his back and gasping for much-needed air. Ben wanted to do the same, but he couldn't. Not yet.

'The canopy!' he shouted to Danny. 'We should rip it down, stop it filling with air.'

Danny nodded and together they started clawing at the fabric. It was tough, though, and difficult to tear. Only when Ben remembered he had a set of keys in his soaking wet jeans did he manage to stab a hole in the fabric. Once that was done, it was much easier to bring down the canopy.

It made an instant difference. The boat still rocked precariously with the force of the water, but at least the canopy wasn't now acting as an out-of-control sail. When Ben, sore and soaking, took the helm, it was by no means easy. But at least it wasn't as difficult as before, and they started making better headway through the howling winds towards the plane.

As they approached the aircraft from the water, they could see that it was still burning and smouldering, as was the grass surrounding it. There was no way they could have passed it by land. The alligators became fewer and fewer, though, the nearer they got to the plane, and it was easy to tell why. Even from the water, and even in the high winds, Ben could feel the heat of the burning aircraft against his skin. It was uncomfortably hot. He manoeuvred the boat away from land and passed the aeroplane at quite some distance.

All of them, he noticed, were staring at the burning plane rather than concentrating on the rocking of the boat in the high winds. It didn't take a rocket scientist to work out that they were all considering what might have been if Ben hadn't landed that thing.

As they passed the plane, Ben snapped himself out of it. He squinted his eyes and looked towards land, trying to see if there was any sign of the other passengers

– or of any gators taking refuge from the rough waters.

'Looks like the other passengers are on the move,' Ben shouted.

Danny and Angelo followed his gaze. 'We should get to land,' Danny replied. 'I don't like being on this boat any longer than we have to. Can you get closer? See if there are any alligators?'

Ben nodded and turned the boat towards the shore.

To their relief, it seemed clear. As they approached the wide marsh road, there was no sign of anything much. Danny reclaimed his shotgun and ammo from under the seat and they jumped awkwardly out of the boat and onto dry land. It felt good for Ben to have his feet on solid ground.

They were silent for a minute as the howling gales blustered around them.

'We need to keep an eye out,' Ben said finally. 'Those gators came out of nowhere, remember.'

The other two nodded seriously as Ben looked east, away from the plane.

He shrugged. 'Other than that,' he said, 'I guess the best we can do is keep moving. Let's see if we can catch up with the others. Come on – let's go.'

Chapter Eleven

The three of them started running down the road. When that became too difficult, they slowed to a fast walk. They were too out of breath to do much talking, and the screaming winds didn't help things.

Surely the weather couldn't get any worse than this. Ben had to keep his eyes half shut to protect them against the flying spray and the other bits of minuscule debris that were flying around. It made the going even trickier.

With every step he took, Ben's half-closed eyes were darting around looking for alligators. The very thought of them sent a shiver down his spine, and he didn't know what on earth they would do if they came across another horde of the beasts. He was vaguely aware of Danny loading the shotgun as he walked alongside him; but a couple of rounds from the gun wouldn't make much difference if the reptiles started swarming like they had done on the other side of the plane.

More than once, he tripped. They all did. It was impossible to stay standing against some of the gusts that were blowing now. Overhead the sky was growing darker, though it was impossible to tell whether that was because night was falling or because the sun was covered with thick, fast-moving clouds. Ben looked at his watch, but it had been damaged by the water and was as good as useless.

They had been travelling for half an hour, maybe more, when Ben stopped.

He cocked his head and listened.

There was a strange noise in the air.

'Hold on!' he shouted at the others.

They stopped. 'What is it?'

'Did you hear that?'

Angelo looked confused. 'Hear what?'

'A kind of . . . *howling*.'

His Italian friend blinked at him, then looked up into the air. 'What are you *talking* about, Ben? We're in the middle of a hurricane. Of *course* I can hear howling.'

But Ben shook his head. 'No,' he said. 'Not that. Something else—'

He stopped short. There it was again. A long, high-pitched wail.

The three of them looked at each other worriedly. There was no doubting that what they had just heard wasn't the wind. It was something quite different.

'We need to keep going,' Danny said tensely. 'Whatever it is, there's no point just standing here.'

Ben found himself wishing they hadn't left the boat. One look out onto the marshland, however, told him that it would be just as dangerous out there as anywhere else. Besides, the chances of the boat still being by the road where they left it were almost zero. Danny was right. They just had to carry on.

It continued to grow darker. Ben found himself shivering. Half of that was because of the wet clothes blown cold against his skin; but half of it was something else. He was scared, obviously. Scared of the hurricane, scared of what might happen when they finally hooked up with the other passengers. But the howling had sent a chill all the way through him. He didn't know what had made the sound, and he didn't want to find out.

Just as that thought went through his head, Danny spoke.

'What's that?' he asked. His voice was taut. Tense.

They stopped, and Ben peered into the distance.

It was about thirty metres away and from this distance it didn't look much bigger than a dog. It wasn't a dog, though – Ben could tell that from its outline. Its ears were pointed and its body was lean and sleek. Ben thought back to the poster he had seen in the wardens' station, and he thought he knew what the animal was.

Before he could say anything, however, Danny was moving. He crouched down flat on the ground and pointed his shotgun in the direction of the animal in front of them. The butt of the weapon was firmly pressed into his shoulder: Ben could tell he was going to shoot any minute.

'No!' he roared. He kicked the barrel of the gun just as Danny fired it. The noise of the shot cracked through the air, but the round discharged itself harmlessly over the marshland.

'What are you doing?' Danny demanded angrily.

'You can't shoot it,' Ben shouted back. 'I think it's a Florida panther. They're incredibly rare.'

'A *panther*?' Angelo demanded. 'Aren't they also incredibly dangerous.'

Ben didn't answer. He looked in the direction of the animal. To his relief, he saw it running in the opposite direction.

'Look.' He pointed. 'It's running away. The noise of the gun must have scared it.' He turned to Danny, who had scrambled to his feet. 'Keep that thing loaded,' he said. 'We might need to scare it off again.'

Danny nodded, but didn't say anything. Ben could tell he was annoyed by what he'd just done, but there was nothing for it. He wasn't going to stand by and let one of these rare animals be killed. Not as long as there was another option. With a deep breath he started moving again and prayed that that was the last they'd seen of the endangered animal.

They were feeling pretty endangered themselves, now. Endangered and terrified. It was getting more and more difficult to walk because of the increasing wind, and now they had panthers to worry about as well as the alligators. It didn't take too long before Danny called them to a halt again.

'Look!' he called. 'Up ahead.'

There were two of them this time, standing on either side of the road like statues at the entrance to a grand house. Despite the high winds, they were perfectly still. The trio stopped and there was a moment of awesome tension as the humans and animals stared at each other.

And then they pounced.

The panthers moved astonishingly quickly. Ben had seen greyhounds racing before, and he was reminded of that.

'Danny!' he warned, but he needn't have. The older man had the shotgun raised. He fired a round into the air. In an instant the Florida panthers screeched to a halt and scampered the opposite way down the road and out of sight.

'How many of them do you think there are?' Angelo asked.

Ben shrugged. 'Dunno,' he said. 'Maybe that's it. Maybe not.'

He turned to Danny, who was already reloading the gun. 'They're going to get used to the sound of the gun, you know, Ben,' the older man said.

Ben didn't reply. There wasn't much to say.

He had his heart in his throat as they carried on down the road. Every time the wind howled – and that was often – Ben felt himself straining his ears to see if it *was* just the wind, or if it was the noise of the big cats ahead. As the minutes passed, he decided that the creatures' calls were definitely becoming more frequent; and although it was difficult to tell one from the other, he also decided that there were several different panthers yowling.

It didn't take long for his eyes to confirm what his ears suspected.

From the gloom ahead, an outline of a pack of panthers appeared. At a glance, Ben couldn't tell how many there were, and he wasn't going to start counting. He found himself rooted to the spot, waiting for the moment that they pounced, as they surely would.

It came soon enough.

The pack moved as one. As they did, Danny stepped in front of Ben and Angelo. 'Stay behind me,' he ordered.

133

'No problem,' Angelo muttered.

The two of them let Danny take the lead.

He let them get close this time – close enough for Ben to have a good look at them. Under different circumstances he knew he would be marvelling at what beautiful creatures they were. The animals were sleek and lean, and their strong muscles rippled under their light brown fur. Their faces were well defined and full of expression: the only problem was that Ben didn't like the expression they were making. They were snarling, and he could see their long, knife-sharp teeth.

'Danny!' he called worriedly. The gun hadn't been fired yet. 'They're getting too close!'

BANG! The shotgun fired. And then a second time. Just as before, the panthers stopped mid-run and started scurrying back. They didn't disappear this time, however. Instead they stopped to regroup much closer to the petrified trio.

Ben squinted his eyes once more. 'What's that?' he shouted. Beyond the animals, almost out of sight but not quite, he thought he saw another building. 'Can you see it? Is it another wardens' station up ahead?'

'I think it is,' Angelo replied breathlessly. 'But how can we get there? We've got to go through the panthers.'

Ben's mind was racing, and it was difficult for him to get his thoughts straight. He closed his eyes and took a deep breath. 'We're going to have to keep moving forward,' he said finally. 'Get as close as we can and then fire a couple of shots. It'll make them move back and we should be able to keep gaining ground.' He turned to Danny. 'What do you think?'

Danny's brow furrowed. 'I think we don't have much choice,' he said grimly. He looked ahead to the panthers. 'Stay behind me,' he instructed before turning to Ben. 'Listen, Ben,' he said. 'I know they're rare and everything, but if they get too close, I'm not going to have any choice but to try and take them out.'

Ben's lips thinned, but he knew the older man was right. He nodded his head in reluctant agreement. 'All right,' he said. 'Let's go.'

They moved slowly. Warily. At first the panthers kept their distance, but as time passed they seemed to become bolder. Ben watched nervously as they regrouped, and it wasn't long before the animals started edging towards them. They moved slowly at first, creeping, as though they were stalking their prey – which in a way, Ben thought to himself glumly, they were.

And then, all as one, as though someone had just started a firing pistol, they upped their pace.

'Keep going!' Danny shouted. The three of them continued their steady walk – or as steady as was possible in the howling gale. Danny had his gun pointed just above the panthers, but for the moment he didn't shoot.

'*Danny!*' Ben urged. 'Now would be a good time—'

Danny shook his head. 'The closer they are, the louder it'll sound to them.'

He held his nerve.

Ben felt his stomach tying up into knots. They were playing a dangerous game. The animals were so close – he could see their sharp teeth.

Suddenly Danny fired the gun. Two rounds cracked in the air and, as before, the panthers screeched to a halt and then scampered back.

'Run!' Danny shouted. 'While they're scared.'

The three of them raced as fast as they could towards the wardens' station. They made surprisingly good time and were only twenty metres away when the panthers started to charge them again.

'I need to reload!' Danny shouted. He broke the shotgun and the spent cartridges flew out. Quickly he fumbled in his rucksack for some new rounds.

'Hurry up, Danny!' Angelo shouted. '*Hurry up!*'

The panthers were powering towards them. To Ben's horror, Danny dropped one of the cartridges on the ground. He bent down to pick it up, but by that time the animals were nearly on them. Ben could hear their snarling over the sound of the wind. It was a low, greedy growl.

It was sheer instinct that made him run, and Angelo did the same. He could hear the patter of the panthers' feet just behind him and any moment he expected them to leap on his back and sink their teeth into his flesh.

And only then did he hear the gun. Another two rounds – and not before time.

Behind him there was a whimper and then the sound of the animals retreating. Ben stopped and looked over his shoulder. Sure enough, the panthers had given up the chase. But for how long, he couldn't tell.

'Get to the wardens' station! *Now!*' Danny roared.

Ben and Angelo didn't need telling twice. Adrenaline surging through their bodies, they sprinted towards the building. As they approached, though, the panthers charged again. The gunshot hadn't sent them running nearly as far, and they seemed emboldened now. They sensed blood.

Ben had never run so fast in his life. His muscles burned as he desperately tried to propel himself towards the building. Danny, being taller, got there first. He crashed the door open and held it for them as Ben and Angelo burst through it. The moment they were safely in, he slammed it shut. As soon as the door was closed, the noise of the hurricane softened slightly; but they could hear the animals, growling and scratching around the outside. If they dared to step out of the building, they'd be panther food.

The three of them were silent for a good couple of

minutes. Angelo lay flat on the ground, his breath coming in short, sharp gasps. Ben was breathing heavily too, his face flushed and his legs like jelly. He was bent double, his hands on his knees, as he tried to regain his energy; Danny was in a similar position.

It was Ben who recuperated first. 'Close shave,' he muttered.

The others didn't respond.

Ben looked around. The wardens' station was very similar to the one they had been in previously – the same layout, and similar posters on the wall. As before there was a picture of a Florida panther – Ben couldn't quite bring himself to look at it this time, or read the words on the poster which no doubt said how rare it was, and how lucky he'd be to see one. Just now, Ben would have been perfectly happy never to see another of those animals as long as he lived.

The windows, he saw with relief, had not been blown in. Not yet, at least. He peered out of one of them. The panthers had not congregated here – they were too busy lurking by the main door. From here, the storm looked even more ferocious than when they were actually out in it. As he watched, it started to rain again, heavy, powerful rain that seemed to sheet down from different directions. Before long, he could barely see the turbulent marsh waters on either side of the road. The raindrops thundered on the roof of the building, almost

– but not quite – drowning out the sound of the wind.

Ben was briefly transfixed by the awesome sight of the storm. And then, peeping round the back of the building, he saw something.

His face lit up.

'Danny!' he called. 'Angelo!'

The two of them turned to look at him. 'What?' Angelo asked, his face full of exhaustion.

'Round the back,' he said. 'I think there's a truck.'

Angelo blinked.

'Look,' Ben continued. 'I can just see its bumper through this window.'

The other two joined him. 'You're right,' Danny said.

The three of them continued to peer out of the window, captivated by the sight of the truck – perhaps their only chance of getting out of here safely. It was as they were staring that Ben noticed something out of the corner of his eye. Danny's gaze was flickering between the truck and Angelo and there was a strange expression on his face. Ben couldn't quite put his finger on it, but whatever it was, it made him uneasy.

Angelo broke the silence. 'How do we get to it?' he asked. 'Because if you think I'm walking out of that door when those panthers are there—'

Danny shook his head. 'Let's see if there's a back entrance. The noise of the rain might distract them.'

His voice was tense. Clutching the shotgun, he disappeared into the back room. When he returned, he still had a serious look on his face. He nodded to the others. 'We can get out that way,' he said. 'I put my ear to the door and couldn't hear the panthers. And with a bit of luck there'll be a key in the truck.'

Ben looked out of the window again. The rain was still sheeting down. 'Do you think it's safe? Driving in this weather, I mean.'

Danny frowned grimly. 'Not really,' he said. 'But if these windows break like the other ones did, those animals are going to get in.'

Angelo nodded his head. 'Don't know about you, Ben,' he said, 'but I'm hungry. I'd rather *eat* dinner than *be* it.'

Ben shrugged. 'All right,' he agreed. 'Let's do it.'

He and Angelo walked towards Danny, who stepped aside to let them into the back room. As Ben passed him, he noticed that the man's hands were shaking. He stopped. 'You all right?'

Danny's face twitched and he seemed not to want to catch Ben's eye. 'Fine,' he replied. 'Just a bit, you know—' He glanced over in the direction of the main door.

'Right,' Ben replied. It was fair enough – they were all spooked by what had just happened. But still something didn't seem quite right. He tried to put the thought from his mind. He was on edge. They all were. They just needed to find the others and get out of the Everglades. Then everything would be all right.

'We should go out one by one,' Danny called as Ben and Angelo approached the back door. 'There might only be one door open. If we crowd round the truck, it'll take us longer to get in, and with those panthers out there—' He pushed past them. 'I'll go first,' he said. 'I'll open the passenger doors. Give me thirty seconds and then Angelo, you go next. Ben, thirty seconds after that. Keep this door shut – we don't want the panthers getting inside. OK?'

The two boys nodded.

'All right then,' Danny said. 'Good luck.' He opened the back door and the room seemed to fill with the howling of the wind and the rain. Swiftly, Danny stepped outside and shut the door behind him.

They waited in silence. Both of them, Ben knew, could feel the tension.

After about thirty seconds, Angelo nodded. 'Go for it,' Ben said quietly, then watched as his Italian friend disappeared out into the elements.

Now Ben was alone. He listened carefully at the door, his ears straining for the sound of the panthers attacking. But there was nothing. Just the noise of the rain and the wind. He tried not to think of what had gone before: the plane, the alligators, the panthers. The poster he had seen spoke of pythons too. That would be the icing on the cake, he thought to himself glumly as he waited for the time to pass.

Then, when the moment arrived, he took a deep breath, opened the door and stepped outside.

At first he was blinded by the rain. Ben barely took in his surroundings as he rushed to the truck. It was a sturdy-looking thing – a pick-up truck, bright red with huge, off-road tyres. There was a front cab, and the back was covered by a thick fabric that was flapping in the wind but seemed robust nevertheless. Ben sprinted to the front passenger door.

It was only when he got there that he realized something was wrong.

He blinked as he looked through the window and checked again that his eyes weren't deceiving him. But there was no doubt about it.

Danny and Angelo weren't there.

A sick feeling went through him. Almost involuntarily he spun round to see what had happened to them. And it was only then that he saw him.

Danny was standing right behind Ben, only a metre away. His hair was blowing in the wind. In his hands he gripped the shotgun. It was not pointing in Ben's direction, but was held by the barrel. Like a bludgeon.

And Danny's face was set, his eyes narrow.

'I'm sorry, Ben,' he said, quietly but without any real

remorse. Without another word he slammed the butt of the gun down on the side of Ben's head.

As he did so, the wind shrieked horribly. It was the last sound Ben heard before he passed out.

Chapter Twelve

When Ben awoke, his head was in agony.

He was lying on his side, his face pressed against something cold and hard. His cheekbone juddered uncomfortably against the surface. Thanks to his grogginess, it was perhaps a minute before he realized that he was travelling in a moving vehicle.

He groaned and tried to put his hands to his head. It was only then that he realized his arms were tied tightly behind his back. He struggled to release them, but without any luck: something was digging deeply and painfully into his wrists, and the more he moved them, the worse it hurt.

It took a supreme effort for him to force his body into a sitting position. Outside the wind was still howling. It made the vehicle shake, which did nothing for the bruises on Ben's body or the pain in his head.

All around him it was dark and gloomy, but he could make out the figure of Angelo, unconscious beside him. His friend was also tied up, and an ugly welt on the side of his face suggested that he had received the same treatment as Ben.

With that thought, Ben remembered Danny. The way he had come up behind him; the implacable look on his face as he raised the butt of his gun and slammed it down on the side of Ben's head. How long ago that had been, Ben couldn't have said; but he worked out that they had to be in the back of the truck. Painfully he turned his head to look towards the front of the vehicle. There, separated from him and Angelo by a pane of glass, was Danny. Their companion was looking straight ahead, clearly focusing on the difficult drive. It was gloomy outside, and the headlamps of the truck illuminated the terrifying way forward. The rain was still sheeting down, and unknown objects were flying around in the air. Danny's gun was resting on the passenger seat next to him. The moment Ben saw it, his mind started working overtime. How could he get his hands on the weapon? How could he get himself and Angelo out of this situation? And what on *earth* was Danny playing at?

Just then, he noticed the older man's eyes flicker in the rear-view mirror. Danny looked momentarily surprised that Ben was up and about, but as their eyes locked his expression soon settled down into that dead-pan look that Ben found so unnerving.

And then, to Ben's surprise, the truck ground to a halt.

Danny grabbed the shotgun and jumped out of the vehicle. Moments later there was the sound of the rear doors unlocking and he appeared at the back of the truck. The gun was pointed directly at Ben.

'You,' Danny said curtly. 'Get out now.'

Ben blinked. There was something different in Danny's voice. Before he had spoken with a perfect American accent, but now there was no hint of it. Instead he spoke his perfectly good English with an accent Ben could not locate.

'What for?' Ben demanded.

'I said, get out.' Danny nodded the gun in Ben's direction, making it clear that there was no option but to do as he was told.

Ben squirmed out of the back of the truck. When his feet hit the ground he nearly fell from the dizziness and his head grew even more painful. A wave of nausea passed over him. As he bent double, Danny grabbed him roughly by the arm and moved him round to the front passenger door, which he opened. 'Get inside,' he barked.

Ben felt himself being pushed up into the cab of the truck and, still dizzy and nauseous, he was unable to struggle as Danny pulled a seat belt around his body – more, he suspected, to stop him from moving than out of a deep concern for his welfare. The man then took his place behind the steering wheel, tucked the gun away by his left-hand side and carried on driving.

It was a couple of minutes before Ben felt well enough to speak. 'Why did you put me in the front?' he whispered hoarsely.

Danny's eyes flickered towards him, but then immediately went back to the road. 'You are a clever boy, Ben,' he replied solemnly. 'Too clever for my liking. I feel more comfortable with you sitting here next to me than thinking of you plotting with—' His lip curled slightly. 'With *him* back there.'

Ben closed his eyes and shook his head. None of this made sense. *None of it.* Danny seemed like he had turned into a different person. In the last couple of hours, Ben and Angelo had saved his life; and he had saved theirs. So what was he doing now? Why had he tied them up? Why did he sound so full of hate?

'Danny,' he rasped. His voice was dry and he realized he was incredibly thirsty. 'I don't know what this is all about but you've got nothing to worry about from me and Angelo. All we want to do is find the others, to warn them about—'

And then he stopped.

He opened his eyes and slowly turned his head

towards the man sitting next to him as an awful realization fell upon him.

'What happened to your American accent?' he asked sharply. And then, as the pieces of the jigsaw started suddenly to fall into place, 'Your name isn't really Danny, is it?'

Danny's eyes narrowed slightly. He didn't reply.

Ben found himself cursing inwardly. 'It's you, isn't it?' he demanded. 'The second terrorist. It's been you all along.'

Danny kept quiet at first. He just kept looking straight ahead, his face emotionless. When he did finally speak, it was slowly and precisely, though still in the accent Ben could not identify. 'If you knew what I was doing,' he said, 'you would understand that it is not the person sitting in the front of this truck that is the terrorist, but the person lying in the back.'

Ben's lip curled, just as he had seen Danny's do. 'Look, Danny,' he spat, 'or whatever your name is. If this is all about Angelo's dad and his business, you should know that there's a difference between the two of them. From what I can tell, I don't think Angelo even likes the guy.'

Danny's face twitched. 'Maybe,' he replied. 'Maybe not. The boy's father, though, has caused untold sorrow to my family. It is only right that he suffers just as we have done.'

'What do you mean?' Ben asked, his face screwed up with confusion. 'What are you *talking* about?'

Danny's eyes flashed. He started to speak, but his voice was drowned out by a sudden howling of the wind that knocked the truck from its course and caused him to concentrate even harder on his driving. Ben's body thumped against the side of the car, and he winced as the ropes that were tying his hands together dug sharply into his bleeding wrists. When the gust had died down, Danny tried again. 'I don't have to explain myself to you,' he stated.

Ben felt anger rising up in him. 'Oh no?' he demanded. 'I saved your life twice today. I reckon that deserves a bit of an explanation, don't you?'

Danny's gaze didn't veer from the road as he negotiated the difficult drive. He snorted. 'I woke up this morning expecting never to see another sunrise. I'm glad I'm still alive, but only because it means that I can see through what I started.'

'And what's that? Tell me, Danny.'

Danny was breathing heavily now, as if he was trying to control his own anger. 'You won't understand.'

'You know what?' Ben asked. 'In the circumstances, I think I'll give it a pretty good go.'

There was a moment of silence between them, broken only by the howling of the wind outside and the struggling of the engine as Danny continued to negotiate the road east. Finally, though, he spoke. 'Very well,' he said. 'I am doing this on account of a young girl, dead because the oil men have raped my people's land.' He spoke with such passion that Ben was forced into silence, and as Danny continued to speak, it was clear that he found what he had to say unbelievably difficult.

'I come from a small island many thousands of miles away from here,' he said emotionlessly. 'You will not have heard of it. There are few who have. We live simple lives, and that makes people in the outside world think we are simple. Stupid. But we are not stupid. We feel things deeply, just like everybody else. We love our land and we mourn the death of our people. For too long now, we have been ignored by the rest of the world, apart from when they want something.' Danny let out a noise that sounded almost like a laugh. 'When that happens, they think they can just take it. Our little island is rich in resources. We choose not to exploit them because we prefer to let the earth be. Some months ago, however, an oil company – the one owned by *his* father – arrived. They ignored our protests and brought in their machines. It was one of those machines that killed the little girl.'

As Danny spoke, Ben found himself transfixed by the man's face. It was difficult to tell with the jolting of the vehicle, but he was sure he could see tears welling up in Danny's eyes.

'There is barely a man among us,' he continued, 'who would not die to see the little girl's death avenged, but I have more reason than most.' He blinked fiercely. 'She was my sister.'

As he said these words, Ben noticed that Danny was gripping the steering wheel of the car so tightly that the whites of his knuckles were showing. Suddenly he swerved to avoid a piece of debris that was flying towards the windscreen of the truck; Ben saw it hurtle past him, only inches away from his side window, before he spoke.

'I'm sorry,' he croaked.

Danny sneered. 'Sorry? What good is it to be sorry? Will that bring back Basheera? Will that stop the suffering of my parents? Of my people?'

Ben drew a deep breath. His captor's voice was full of anger and hatred. He knew he had to choose his words carefully. 'No,' he replied, his voice quiet and uncertain. 'No, it won't. But neither will this – whatever *this* is.'

'*This*,' Danny spat, 'is revenge. And a warning to the rest of the world that they cannot continue to treat us in this way.'

'But I still don't understand,' Ben replied. 'If you wanted to make an example of Angelo, if you wanted to' – he hesitated for a moment – 'to kill him, you've had loads of chances. But you haven't been doing that. You've been helping us. You've been *saving* us.' As he spoke, Ben felt a surge of hope. Maybe Danny was in two minds; maybe he couldn't bring himself to do what he felt he had to do.

But that hope was instantly crushed.

'You don't get it, do you?'

Ben stared at Danny, his stomach tied up in knots again, and shook his head.

Danny's face remained stony hard. 'The hijacking. That was our main plan. We were to fly the plane directly into the oil refinery. It would be on every television screen in the world, and when we let it be known that the son of the refinery owner was on the plane, the plight of my sister would be known by every-one.' His eyes narrowed again. 'We were not expecting the hurricane, and so we had to move fast. Everything went perfectly, until you got involved.'

He glanced meaningfully at Ben. Ben jutted his chin out and stared back.

'Of course, we always knew our plan was risky; we always knew there was a chance it would not work. That's why I remained in the cabin. In the event that we landed safely, I was to apprehend Angelo and carry out the second part of our plan.'

'And what's that?' Ben demanded.

Danny looked as if he was considering whether to reply. In the end he shrugged, as if to say, What harm can come of it? 'My aim since then has been to get

Angelo safely to the oil refinery. That is where we are headed now. We have bought the services of a—' Danny searched for the word, the first time Ben had seen his English falter all day. 'A mercenary. As we speak, he is planting explosive devices at the refinery. When we get there, he will make a videotape of Angelo tied up. After the explosion, he will distribute the videotape to news outlets worldwide, while I let them know why this has happened.' He glanced over at Ben once more. 'Angelo's father has done terrible things to us, Ben,' he whispered. 'The world must see how he pays the price.'

Even as Danny spoke, Ben felt the words 'You're insane' forming on his lips. He kept quiet, however – some kind of sixth sense told him that would be a very bad thing to say to Danny, especially now. Instead he asked the question that was burning in his mind.

'What about me?'

Danny's face twitched. 'You're in the wrong place at the wrong time,' he said. He sounded genuinely regretful.

Sounds like the story of my life, Ben thought to himself. He didn't say it out loud, though. His mind was working overtime as he tried to think of a way to get out of the car, to raise the alarm and stop all this from happening. 'You haven't got any argument with me,' he said. 'Why don't you just let me out? Whatever you have to do with Angelo doesn't need to involve me – I hardly even know the guy.'

Danny smiled a sad little smile. 'Nice try, Ben,' he said quietly. 'But you're too resourceful for me to let you go free. You might even have escaped the panthers if I'd left you back there. So I decided to bring you with me. You've been a good friend to Angelo over the past few hours. And it's only right that good friends should be together at the end, isn't it?'

Ben blinked as the implication of what Danny was saying sank in.

'I'm sorry, Ben,' Danny continued without looking at him. 'You shouldn't really have to die. But I can't risk you messing this up. You'll be with Angelo when the refinery blows. You don't need to worry about it. It'll be quick and painless. The explosion's going to be very, *very* big. It will all be over for you in a second.'

And with that, Danny increased the speed of the pick-up, his face a picture of concentration as he negotiated the road and the storm and tried to keep the truck from being blown from side to side in the howling, powerful gales.

Chapter Thirteen

As far as he could tell, the refinery was completely deserted now. He was glad he had taken the worker's uniform, however, because the yellow hard hat protected his head from the debris flying dangerously around in the terrifyingly strong winds. Even so, he had to keep his head down and his forearm across his eyes in order to move further into the metal jungle with any kind of safety.

The noise of the wind seemed to bounce off the huge metal towers and canisters that surrounded him. It was as though there were sirens all around him, shrieking impossibly loudly, warning him not to go any further. 'Danger!' the gales seemed to shout. '*Danger!*' The mercenary put that fanciful thought from his mind. He was here to do a job. It would have been a lot easier without the storm, but he wasn't going to let a freak of the weather get in his way. He'd only received half his money so far; the rest was payable when the refinery became a fireball. He had to make sure that happened; and he had to make sure he was a long way from there when it did. A long way away and a good deal richer – as soon as the tapes reached the media. He concentrated on that one thought as he pushed onwards.

He was in a covered area now, its vaulted roof supported by huge metal girders. The wind still blew through it, but it was a little less severe. He didn't slow his pace, however. The whole structure was creaking ominously, as though its skeleton was being pushed to breaking point. It was almost a relief to get back out into the open air. Ahead of him, looming in the near-distance, was a large container tower, bigger than the rest, dominating this part of the immense refinery like a skyscraper in the middle of a village. He grunted in satisfaction: this was where he was headed. The first device needed to be placed against the shell of this tower to cause maximum devastation. He would be destroying others, too, but this was the important one.

Minutes later he was at the base of the tower. A metal ladder stretched up to the top of it, but before he climbed that he needed to prepare the device. He sheltered as best he could from the wind behind the wall of a small Portakabin, then opened his bag and felt inside.

He had five blocks of C-4 plastic explosive in his bag, each of them weighing 500 grams. They were small – not much bigger than a bar of soap – but it was a powerful variety and he knew it would be enough to rip through the shell of the oil container. Once that happened, of course, the thing would go up like a rocket. He pulled out one of the blocks, then fished around for one of the tiny fuses he had carefully constructed the previous day. The fuse itself was only a little bigger than the block of plastic explosive: a black metal box with two sharp prongs sticking out of it. Inside there was a powerful magnet and an electronic receiver – small, but with a long range. It needed to be, if he was going to get far enough away to activate the fuse remotely.

Once the device was prepared, he clutched it firmly in his hand and approached the ladder.

The mercenary didn't need to climb too high, but it was still a precarious business as he clutched the ladder with one hand, the device with the other and braved the powerful winds that almost seemed to be *trying* to knock him off. By the time he reached the bottom of the canister, he was sweating profusely and his muscles ached from the exertion. He held on tight as he stretched out the hand which held the bomb and clamped the device firmly to the metal of the massive canister. To his satisfaction, the device stuck fast. He clutched the ladder with both hands and slowly, carefully, climbed back down.

One down. Four to go. Everything was proceeding according to plan. He turned his back on the main tower and went in search of the remaining locations.

Danny and Ben travelled in silence. There wasn't much more to say.

Night was beginning to fall and the pick-up's headlamps shone brightly. They illuminated the bits of vegetation and who knows what else that were swirling ahead of them, as well as lighting up the road. At one point, Ben was convinced he saw the huge cylindrical shape of a massive snake crawling over a fallen tree. A python? He shuddered. He vaguely wondered too what had happened to the cabin crew and other passengers from the plane. He had seen no sign of them as they drove towards the outside edges of the Everglades. He supposed they had found transport out, like themselves, but he didn't really dwell on the question. There were more pressing matters now, after all.

Every now and then he glanced over his shoulder into the back of the truck. Angelo was still unconscious. Danny must have hit him pretty hard – Ben's Italian friend was going to know about it when he finally woke up. When that happened, Ben was going to need a plan. Angelo would find out soon enough what Danny had in store for him, but as the truck struggled through the winds Ben decided that it would be better to put off telling him for as long as possible. Angelo was a good guy, and brave in his way; but he had a tendency to panic and that was the last thing they needed if they were going to try and get out of this. No, Ben thought to himself. He would try to keep quiet about his friend's potential fate.

After a little while – Ben couldn't have said how long – they reached the eastern entrance to the park. A huge billboard bore a cheerful greeting, but it had been knocked over in the wind and now lay on its back. There were a few low buildings here and there, but the whole area was deserted. Ben briefly considered trying to break out of the truck, but he soon put that thought from his mind. He was the only one who knew what Danny was planning to do to Angelo; and even if his friend's life hadn't been in danger, he had to stop this man from carrying out his threat to blow up the refinery. It would be devastating at the best of times; but in the middle of a hurricane, who could tell what sort of pandemonium it would cause. Ben didn't know where the oil refinery was, but he knew it could well be situated near a populated area. And if the fire spread . . .

He shuddered as memories of Adelaide flickered

through his brain. He *had* to do something to stop this. He *had* to.

As if called into his field of vision by the thoughts that were going through Ben's head, a huge road sign approached. 'Florida City' it announced. '9 miles.' Ben blinked, then turned to Danny.

'The refinery,' he asked. 'Is it far from Florida City?'

Danny shook his head. 'Just south,' he replied. 'But we need to get into town to approach it.' He looked over at Ben. 'Don't try anything stupid, Ben. I've still got the shotgun by my side, remember.'

As if I'm likely to forget, Ben felt like saying. And then his brow furrowed as a thought struck him. If Danny had the gun all along, and if he wanted Ben out of the way, why hadn't he just shot him back at the wardens' station? Why was he taking the risk of having to get Ben to the refinery when all it could do was make life more difficult for him. Could it be that Danny, despite all his hard words, did not have the stomach to kill Ben in cold blood? Could it be that there was a chink in his captor's armour? Ben stowed that possibility away in his mind, ready to use it should the opportunity arise.

The wind was still screaming outside, causing the palm trees that lined the road to bend as though they were made of rubber. Signs of the devastation the wind had caused were everywhere: abandoned cars turned over onto their sides, broken-in windows of deserted houses, fences all but obliterated; trees felled. At first the road remained clear, but as they sped away from the Everglades towards Florida they started seeing more traffic. The cars were few and far between at first, but after a couple of miles they became increasingly numerous. Ben had half expected to see lines of traffic heading out in one particular direction, evacuating the area; but in fact the vehicles seemed to be taking all sorts of routes. He had the sense that the people driving them were in a panic. He didn't blame them.

Somehow, however, he didn't share their panic, though he had enough reason to. He felt numb to it: numb to the wind and to the danger; numb to the horrific scenario that awaited him. For some reason he heard Alec's voice echoing in his head. *You're a brave lad, Ben. But you can't go round the world saving everyone, you know.*

Ben clenched his jaw. Alec was probably right. But sometimes you didn't have a choice. Sometimes saving everyone and saving yourself went hand in hand, and there was no way Ben was going to sit back and let disaster come to him. He wasn't going down without a fight.

'You can't do this, you know,' he told Danny, struggling to make his voice heard above the wind. 'It's madness. To set fire to an oil refinery on the edge of a populated area – think of the consequences. Think how many people could be killed, especially if the winds make the fire spread.'

Danny said nothing.

'Trust me,' Ben persisted urgently. 'I've been around one bad fire. It's not the sort of thing you'd want on your conscience.'

Danny's face remained emotionless. 'My conscience is clear,' he said shortly. 'My conscience—'

But he didn't finish his sentence, because at that moment there was a massive crashing sound as something flew directly into the windscreen. Ben tried to throw his arms over his face to protect himself, but all he managed to do was make the ropes dig in more; Danny did the same thing, and immediately he lost control of the truck.

Everything was a blur: the darkness outside, the headlamps, the shattered glass. Ben could barely see what was happening, but he could feel it sure enough. The pick-up veered towards the side of the road, then suddenly stopped with a sickening crunch. Ben was thrown forward violently; he was only stopped from flying through the shattered windscreen by the seatbelt that locked him firmly in place. It hurt, though, as the whiplash cracked through his body, and he thought he could feel bits of glass prickling over his skin.

The wind continued to howl, but between Ben and Danny there was a moment of silence. In front of them was a palm tree. They had driven into it and the front of the pick-up was completely crushed. Ben looked towards his captor. A shard of glass had sliced one side of the man's face, but Danny barely seemed to notice it. Instead he was looking round, as if trying to work out what he was going to do now.

'Angelo!' Ben shouted suddenly. 'We need to check he's all right. He's not strapped in. He could have been really hurt.' He looked back over his shoulder into the rear of the vehicle, but it was too dark now to see his friend.

Danny's face flickered as he undid his seatbelt and grabbed the shotgun. 'You,' he said shortly, his voice slightly less sure of itself than it had been during their car journey. 'Stay there. Any heroics . . .' He looked meaningfully at the gun. It was clear what he meant. Ben's captor jumped out of the truck and he heard him opening the rear doors of the pick-up.

Ben's mind was doing somersaults as the wind roared through the windscreen. He half closed his eyes to protect them. This felt like a chance, but he didn't know what he could do. His hands were tied and Danny had a gun. Maybe his best bet was just to jump out and try and flag down a car. But who would stop for them in the middle of a hurricane?

His silent question was immediately answered as his eyes were suddenly blinded by the headlamps of a vehicle approaching. He couldn't tell what sort of car it was, but as he vaguely made out the silhouette of a person coming towards him, he felt a massive wave of relief. Whoever it was had their coat pulled up over their head and was moving quickly, as though they didn't want to stay out in the open air too long. It was a man, Ben saw as he approached the passenger side window, with a beard – but that was all he could tell. He rapped on the glass. 'You OK in there?' he screamed. 'You need help?'

Ben nodded his head furiously. 'Open the door!' he yelled over the wind. 'I'm tied up – I can't do it?'

Ben's words obviously sounded strange to the man, because a look of confusion crossed his face. 'Tied up?' he asked. 'What do you mean, tied up?'

Ben opened his mouth to answer, but the words never left him. Because just then he saw the tip of Danny's shotgun appear outside the passenger window and press against the side of the bearded man's skull.

The man froze.

'Very slowly, give me your car keys, and get on the floor,' Danny shouted, his hair blowing wildly in the wind.

The man's eyes flickered between Danny and Ben, but he had no option other than to do as he was told. He slowly lowered the coat that was covering his head, handed over some keys and then hit the ground.

Danny opened the door of the pick-up. 'Get out,' he told Ben curtly. Ben struggled from the truck, jumping over the terrified man, who was lying just by it, his hands on his head. He realized that Danny was now training the gun on him. 'He's awake,' he said shortly. 'Help him out of the back and take him to this guy's car.'

'I can't do anything with my hands tied,' Ben shouted.

Danny's eyes narrowed momentarily. 'Turn round,' he said. Ben did as he was told, and he felt his captor untying the knot that was binding him. It was an untold relief to have his hands free, but the sense of relief didn't last long because immediately Danny put the gun to his head. 'I mean what I say, Ben. Try anything and I'll shoot.' Danny was shouting, but that didn't stop his voice trembling slightly.

Ben cast him an ugly look but nodded his head in obedience. Then he walked round to the back of the truck. The doors were open and Angelo was sitting with his legs dangling out of the back. The Italian boy was a mess. His hands were tied behind his back just like Ben's had been and he had obviously been thrown around a lot when the pick-up crashed. His face was bruised and bleeding and he had a distant, pained look in his eyes. He looked up at Ben and it seemed to take a moment for him to realize who he was.

'Ben,' he croaked finally. '*Che succede?* What's going on? Why am I tied up?'

Ben took a deep breath before replying. 'It's Danny,' he said as quietly as he could while still being heard over the wind. 'He's, er . . . he's not quite who we thought he was.'

Angelo's face screwed up in concentration as he tried to process that piece of information. 'What do you mean?'

Ben chose his words carefully. 'You remember what Brad said? About there being a second terrorist on the plane? It's him.'

Angelo shook his head groggily. 'That doesn't make sense. Danny's been—'

He didn't finish, because suddenly Danny reappeared, holding the bearded man at gunpoint. 'Get in the truck,' he ordered his new hostage.

As the man climbed into the back of the crashed pick-up, Danny pulled Angelo out. The Italian's knees buckled, but he just about managed to stand as the doors of the pick-up were slammed shut and locked, trapping the bearded man inside. Then Danny waved the gun in Ben's direction once more. 'The car,' he shouted. 'Now.'

Ben took Angelo's arm and helped him walk, using his other arm to shield their faces. As they approached the vehicle, its headlights still glowing in the darkness,

Ben saw it was another pick-up, though this time the rear of it was not covered with a canopy and was exposed to the elements. He directed Angelo round to the passenger side, opened the door and helped him in, all the while aware that Danny had his gun firmly pointed at his back.

Once Angelo was safely in the new truck, Ben started to climb in. As he did, however, he felt Danny's hand on his shoulder, pulling him back.

'Not you,' Danny instructed.

Ben turned round. Danny was still pointing the gun at him, but in his other hand he held the car keys up.

'I can't keep an eye on you both if I'm driving,' he instructed. 'You'll have to do it. Take the keys.'

'I don't know how to drive,' Ben lied.

Danny raised a disbelieving eyebrow. 'You can fly a plane, but you can't drive a car? I don't think so, Ben.' He nudged the gun against Ben's shoulder. 'Take the keys,' he repeated.

Ben looked around him. The wind was worse than ever and he really didn't know if he was going to be able to keep control of the truck. Still, it didn't look like he had much choice. Reluctantly, he took the keys from Danny's fist and walked round to the other side of the truck. He opened the door and climbed in.

By the time Ben was settled behind the wheel, Danny was sitting in the far-side passenger seat with

Angelo, bruised and bleary and with his hands still tied behind his back, between them. Their captor had his body half twisted towards Ben; the shotgun, which he held firmly, stretched across Angelo's torso and was pointed directly at Ben. 'There are two rounds in here, Ben,' Danny reminded him. 'It only takes one to kill you.'

Again, the thought flashed through Ben's mind: if Danny was prepared to kill him, why hadn't he done so yet? Was he really up to it?

It wasn't a question, though, that he really wanted to put to the test. Nor did Danny give him the chance to do so.

'Drive,' he said curtly. 'Now.'

Chapter Fourteen

Controlling the truck was more difficult than Ben could have imagined.

It took several false starts before he got going and started to grow used to the feel of the pedals. Once they were moving, it felt for all the world as if there were people outside trying to knock the vehicle over. It was just the wind, of course, but no less scary for that. The rain had started up again – huge, pellet-like drops that slammed against the windscreen causing a flood of water that the windscreen wipers barely had a chance to scrape away. He felt as if he would be unable to keep the truck going in a straight line for any period of time, but somehow, with all his effort, he managed it.

They travelled the main highway into Florida City. None of the road lights were lit, and all the buildings they passed had also been plunged into darkness. Ben assumed the storm had caused some sort of power outage. The roads became busier and Ben found that sweat was dripping down his forehead as he concentrated on the road ahead. More than once he considered crashing the truck on purpose; but one look at the shotgun pointed in his direction soon put him off. It wouldn't take much for the loaded weapon to go off accidentally and the barrel was pointing straight at him. Occasionally Danny uttered a curt instruction, telling him which way to go. He seemed to know these streets well, and Ben really had no choice other than to do as his captor said.

They had been going for about ten minutes when, seemingly on an impulse, Danny switched the car radio on. A blank crackle came from the truck's speakers as he twisted the dialling knob to try and find a station. It took a while – clearly many of the stations were down because of the storm – but after a minute or so a voice, indistinct but just about understandable, came over the airwaves. Ben struggled to hear what the urgent voice was saying over the noise of the car engine and the storm outside.

'*This is an emergency broadcast. All residents of southern Florida who have not yet evacuated the area are now advised to take refuge in low-rise buildings. Repeat, all residents of southern Florida who have not yet evacuated the area are advised to seek shelter in buildings of less than two storeys. This is an extreme storm warning. Hurricane Jasmine has made landfall. The National Hurricane Centre has labelled this a Category 5 hurricane. Wind speeds are in excess of 160 miles per hour and a state of emergency has been declared. In addition, Hurricane Jasmine has spawned a severe tornado, category F3, currently approaching the south-eastern Florida area. It is fast-moving and extremely destructive. A tornado of this severity has the ability to tear the roofs off buildings, which is why we advise remaining in low-rise shelters. The storms are predicted to last another twelve hours. Updates will continue to be broadcast on this frequency.'*

There was a pause, and then the broadcast started to repeat itself.

'You hear that?' Ben shouted accusingly at Danny. 'A tornado. This is madness, Danny. It can't happen.'

'Just keep driving,' Danny instructed. 'Turn right here. The road will take you out of Florida City and towards the refinery.'

His words were uncompromising, but the tone of his voice wasn't. He sounded unsure of himself. Unsettled. This was not, Ben sensed, going the way he thought it would. Maybe now was the time to act, to jump on Danny's insecurity. Ben started to speak, but he was interrupted by Angelo. Until now, the Italian boy had simply sat there in shocked silence, gazing expression-lessly out of the window. When he spoke, though, it was with a sudden passion. 'Does anybody want to tell me what's going on here?'

Ben shot a glance over at Danny and imperceptibly shook his head. The truth, he knew, was too much for Angelo to handle at the moment. If Ben was going to do anything to stop Danny, the last thing he needed was his Italian friend panicking. Much better for him to give his own version of the events to come.

'Danny's got a little plan,' he shouted without taking his eyes from the road. 'He still wants to make your father's oil refinery go bang. The fact that we managed to stop the plane from doing it hasn't really put him off.'

Angelo looked aghast at Danny. '*Non capisco*,' he breathed. 'I don't understand why you would do such a thing.'

Danny's lip curled. 'Weren't you listening on the plane?' Then he shook his head, as though the question he had asked was a stupid one. 'Of course you don't understand,' he muttered. 'Nobody understands. What is the phrase you people have? Out of sight, out of mind. The island of my people is a long way from here. Why would you care what happens there?'

'You might find we care more than you think, Danny,' Ben yelled. 'Angelo, the little girl who died. It was Danny's sister.'

Angelo's eyes widened. He seemed lost for words.

'You know, Danny,' Ben continued, 'Angelo isn't his father. I think we can safely say he's as shocked as anyone else by what we've all learned today. You're right – your sister shouldn't have died. But this isn't the way to deal with it. It's not going to bring her back.'

'*Shut up!*' Danny screamed. '*Just shut up!*'

A silence.

And then, as if he could not hold back the flood of emotions, 'I know it will not bring her back. That is not the purpose of what we are doing.'

'Then what is?' Ben demanded. 'Just what *is* the purpose, Danny?'

'To make the world understand that we cannot be treated like this. That there are more important things than your precious oil. And, yes, revenge. To make Angelo's father feel the pain that my own parents are suffering.'

Ben swerved the truck sharply to avoid something that was hurtling along the road towards them. As he straightened up again, Angelo spoke. 'So you mean to kill me,' he asked quietly. 'That is why you are taking me to the refinery.'

Danny nodded curtly, and Ben noticed that he avoided Angelo's eye. He took a deep breath, worried about what Angelo's reaction to this new information would be. Angelo, however, seemed to be taking it calmly. He nodded his head, as though accepting something he could not change. 'My father was always worried that something like this would happen,' he announced. 'I guess he always knew that his business interests harmed lots of people.' He turned to Danny and gave him a hard stare. 'But you don't know him,' he said. 'This will not stop him. It will just make him angry. It will be like the opening shot of a war – a war you cannot win.'

Danny scowled. 'Quiet,' he ordered. He shook the barrel of the gun at Ben who, as Angelo had been speaking, had gradually slowed the truck down. 'Keep driving,' he said. 'Faster.'

As Ben put his foot on the accelerator, there was a sound inside the truck – five short beeps, like an alarm clock going off. Ben took his eye off the road momentarily to see what it was: there was nothing on the dashboard and for a second he was perplexed. To his astonishment, however, he saw Danny start to un-button his shirt with his free hand. Strapped to his chest was a leather pouch: when the beeping repeated itself, it was clear that this was where it was coming from. Danny opened the pouch and removed a small plastic case, which he opened. He pulled out what looked like a mobile phone, only bigger and slightly thicker. It beeped for a third time.

Ben snapped his attention back to the road. But at the same time he wondered how the little device could have survived Danny's spell in the water. The plastic case must have been waterproof, he decided. 'What's that?' he demanded.

'A telephone.'

'It won't work,' Ben said. 'We tried, remember? The phone lines are down.'

'It's a satellite phone,' Danny replied as he used the device's small keyboard to type a message with one hand, all the while keeping his gun firmly trained on Ben.

'You mean you had that all the time we were stranded in the Everglades?' Angelo asked acidly. He received no reply from Danny, who just continued to type his message. When he had finished, he carefully packaged the phone up, first into its plastic case and then back into its carrying pouch.

'We're not far,' he announced. 'We should see the refinery up ahead any time soon.'

And with that the three of them fell into a deep, uncomfortable silence.

It was the final explosive device that had given him trouble.

He was soaked now from the constant rain, but that was all right: everything had gone perfectly up until then. The first four devices were firmly attached to their targets, and as the refinery was deserted he hadn't come across anyone to hinder him in his plans. It was as he was climbing the ladder to the final tower, however, that the winds knocked him off. Even as he fell he cursed himself for not holding on more tightly, but with the bomb in one hand, climbing the ladder was always going to be a difficult business.

He fell about five metres. Well-trained, he managed to land in such a way that, while it certainly hurt, it didn't cause any serious injury. But it was with a sick feeling, however, that – just before he hit the ground – he realized he had let go of the bomb. The moment he was on the ground he closed his eyes, then covered his head with his hands. *As if that's going to do any good*, he told himself. If the device accidentally detonated that close to him, he'd be a goner; and if it ignited any part of the refinery, he'd make Guy Fawkes look like a snowman.

He held his breath.

Nothing. Just the constant screaming of the winds. For the first time that day the storm began to rile the mercenary. It wasn't like him – normally he was so cool, so calm. But *when* would the storm be over? He didn't much relish having to escape from the area of the refinery under these conditions.

He looked up. The device was lying a few metres away. The plastic explosive had come away from the fuse and was lying in the rain, harmless for now. He pushed himself up to his feet and retrieved the two parts of the device, carefully drying the prongs of the fuse before reinserting them into the C-4. Then he looked up at the tower again, a determined look on his rain-soaked face. He wasn't going to let the wind get the better of him a second time, and without any further hesitation, he strode up to the ladder and started to climb again.

The rungs were slippery, and the wind was as strong as ever. But he held fast and within a minute the device had been attached. With a sense of relief – and with both hands now available to cling onto the ladder – he descended.

Job done.

He looked around for a place of shelter. Over at the other side of the tower there was an articulated lorry. He ran towards it, opened the passenger door and climbed into the dry cab. His clothes were soaked and the vehicle was being buffeted alarmingly by the winds; even so, it felt good to be out of the elements for a little while. He opened his bag and pulled out the small plastic case holding his satellite communicator. Switching it on, he started typing a message:

DEVICES PRIMED. INFORM ME OF YOUR STATUS.

He sent the message and then waited.

177

As he sat there, the mercenary considered the events of the past few hours. He had been informed that the plane containing his employer's targets had been infiltrated and had kept tabs on the progress of the aircraft using his surveillance systems. When the flight had disappeared from his screens, he assumed that the plane had gone down. But his employers wanted the refinery to be blown up with or without the boy in it, so he had gone ahead with his business. None of them could have predicted these storms, but he wasn't going to let that get in the way of a pay day.

He was a methodical man. Painstaking. He left nothing to chance. He had seen the plane disappear from his surveillance screen, but he had not yet received any confirmation that it had crashed. That was why he was sending his message. He would give the man calling himself Danny five minutes to respond. If not, he would have to assume he was dead. The mercenary would not mourn him – he'd just carry on with his job regardless.

He sat in silence, listening to the wind outside and imagining how he was going to spend his money when all this was over.

And then his satellite communicator beeped.

The mercenary's eyes widened. He hadn't expected this. He hadn't expected it at all. For all his Western ways, he had Danny down as a savage, a refugee from some distant land he had neither heard of nor cared about. How he had managed to survive a plane crash like that was beyond him. He looked down at the screen of the communicator.

EXPECT US WITHIN HALF AN HOUR. ITALIAN BOY IS INTACT. THERE IS ONE OTHER HOSTAGE. ADVISE RENDEZVOUS POINT.

The mercenary shook his head in disbelief. There was more to this guy than he imagined. He had fully expected to leave the refinery without the inconvenience of having to deal with his hostage. But now there was not one hostage, but two. He narrowed his eyes and sat there for a good few minutes while he collected his thoughts and constructed a plan. Finally he typed another message.

TAKE MAIN ROAD INTO REFINERY. THE SITE IS DESERTED BUT DO NOT LET YOUR GUARD DOWN. DON'T LOOK FOR ME — I WILL FIND YOU.

He sent the message and closed the communicator. It seemed like this was going to be more complicated than he thought. But that was OK. He could deal with it. The devices were ready – all he had to do was take delivery of the hostages, make sure they couldn't escape and then put enough distance between himself and the explosion to ensure that he wouldn't be harmed by the scenes of absolute devastation that would most surely follow.

Ben, Angelo and Danny were well outside Florida City now. The roads had once again become deserted. All was dark thanks to the power outages, the wind was slamming blindingly against the windscreen and Ben's tired arms were hurting from the effort of keeping the car on the road. He was desperate to stop, but he knew Danny wouldn't have it: the shotgun pointed directly at him made that perfectly clear.

Suddenly, however, there was a gust of wind that blew him completely off course. He slammed the brakes on to stop the truck veering into the side of the road that was shrouded in darkness. The vehicle skidded and turned a quarter circle on the wet road, coming to a sudden stop.

'What are you doing?' Danny yelled. His voice was a strange mixture of fury and panic. 'Keep driving.'

'I'm trying to stop us crashing, OK?' Ben shouted out. 'The winds are too strong – can't you feel what they're doing to the truck?'

It was a fair enough point. The vehicle was rocking from side to side.

'Anyway,' Ben continued, 'it's hard work driving this

thing. My arms are in agony. I need a rest, otherwise we're not going to make it.'

Ben was just trying to buy time, and Danny could obviously tell. He looked at Ben suspiciously, and Ben fully expected him to force him to keep driving. But for some reason he didn't.

'You've got two minutes,' he said curtly. 'Then we carry on.'

Ben nodded grimly, then edged the truck to the side of the road. When the vehicle came to a halt again, there was an awkward silence. Ben tried to clear his mind. There was no way he and Angelo could fight their way out of this situation – not while Danny had a fully loaded shotgun. All he could do was try and talk their captor round, to appeal to a better nature that he was sure lurked somewhere under the surface.

Angelo had clearly come to the same conclusion, because it was he who broke the silence.

'I can speak to my father,' he announced, his voice frightened, desperate – yet somehow determined. 'He will listen to me. I can get him to make amends.'

Danny sneered. 'Unless he can bring people back from the dead, there are no amends your father can possibly make.'

Angelo looked down at his lap, crestfallen.

Ben breathed deeply. He was only going to get one shot at this, and now was the time. 'Tell me,

Danny,' he asked. 'How come your English is so good?'

Danny looked confused by the question, but he answered it anyway. 'I have lived and worked in America for many years, always sending money back to my family. I have always longed to return, but I will do anything to make sure that they are well.'

Ben nodded with satisfaction. 'Years?' he repeated. 'I suppose, over that time, you've met quite a lot of people.'

Danny shrugged. 'Some.'

'Ordinary people. People with children.'

Danny didn't reply.

'They're the people you're going to harm, Danny, if you go through with this. You know that, don't you?'

Again, Danny kept silent.

'If that oil refinery blows, Danny,' he persisted, 'who knows how many people will die? The winds will make the fire spread. Perhaps even worse, they will spread the smoke. Smoke kills people. They may not die today, or even tomorrow, but it *will* kill them, Danny. Just ordinary families. Families with children.'

He paused.

'Children, Danny. Like your sister.'

Danny was breathing deeply now, and his breath was shaking as though he was trying to keep control over some pent-up emotion. *He's got doubts*, Ben thought to himself. *He doesn't know if he can go through with it.*

A particularly fierce gust hit the truck. They jolted in their seats and Ben waited for it to pass before he continued.

'You can stop this happening, Danny. You're the only one in the world who can stop it from happening. Think of the lives you could save.'

Another pause. Danny's face was stony-still.

'It's in your hands, Danny. It's all in your hands.'

Both Ben and Angelo were staring intently at their captor now, and he seemed unwilling to catch their eye. For a few brief seconds, Ben was deaf to the sound of the winds and the rain outside. Adrenaline pumped through him as he waited for Danny to speak.

But Danny didn't speak. Not yet. Instead, his communicator beeped. It sounded unnaturally loud as it punctured the silence in the car. Danny fumbled for the device and, without changing his blank expression, read the message that had just come through.

He gazed at it, and his breathing remained heavy.

'*Think of the lives you could save, Danny,*' Ben repeated hoarsely.

And then, slowly, Danny turned to look at him. His face was set, and he fixed Ben with a determined steely expression.

'Drive,' he said. 'Drive now. If you say another word, I'll shoot you.'

Chapter Fifteen

Russell Tracey couldn't sleep.

The grey light of morning was beginning to come to Macclesfield. He rolled over in bed and looked at the digital clock on the table next to him. 4.03 a.m. He sighed. There was no way he was going to nod off now. His wife, Bel, lay beside him. Ex-wife, actually, but since Russell's brush with death in the Congo, they'd been making a go of things. For Ben's sake, they had said at first; but as time passed they had realized it was for their sake as well.

Ben. The thought of his son brought a faint smile to Russell's face. He'd be home in a couple of days, and they were both looking forward to him coming back. Neither of them slept well when he wasn't under their roof. He was an independent lad, though, who had proved enough times that he was able to look after himself. They had to allow him his freedom, allow him to spread his wings bit by bit. The holiday with Alec in Grand Cayman was a good way of doing that.

4.04 a.m. Sleep seemed like only a distant possibility now. Quietly, so as not to disturb his slumbering wife, he climbed out of bed, put on his dressing gown and slippers and padded downstairs.

Russell liked the early morning. He liked the stillness. The dawn chorus was just beginning, and looking out of the kitchen window he felt like he had the world to himself. Leisurely, he set about making a cup of tea; as the kettle boiled he switched on the radio.

At first he winced. It sounded like there was some kind of interference in the background and the urgent shouting of the World Service correspondent grated against his ears. He nearly switched off, but then he realized that it wasn't interference he was hearing, it was wind and rain; and what the correspondent had to say grabbed his attention and made his eyes widen.

'*Meteorological experts are calling this the worst storm since records began. Wind speeds of up to 200 miles per hour have been recorded and we've had unconfirmed reports that an aircraft originating from Grand Cayman and bound for Miami has disappeared from air traffic screens. The intensity of the hurricane has made it impossible for search and rescue teams to approach the area.*'

A sensation of cold dread crept through Russell's limbs: the dread that only a parent who fears for their child can know. Ben wasn't *supposed* to be on a flight out of Grand Cayman yet, but Russell knew that feeling of dread wouldn't go away until he was sure that his son was safe. Without turning the radio off, he rushed into the front room and switched the TV on. The news channel was full of images that made his heart stop. Palm trees bent sideways; huge, surging waves crashing over ocean-side roads; cars blown over and house roofs collapsed.

'*US authorities have ordered the evacuation of large parts of south-eastern Florida,*' a voice announced over the images of devastation, '*but scenes of panic are rife in many of the main urban areas. Weather centres are reporting that Hurricane Jasmine has spawned a tornado which made landfall just before sunset this evening and . . . yes . . .*' The reporter hesitated. '*Yes . . . I understand we have just received amateur footage of the tornado now.*'

The screen flickered before being filled again with a blurry image. At first it was impossible to see what the footage showed – it was out of focus and indistinct – but then the picture suddenly sharpened.

Russell blinked. He could barely believe his eyes.

The tornado was out at sea and it looked like a huge, black, spinning wheel with an impossibly long spindle. The sky around it was stormy and the twister was sucking up huge swathes of the ocean and spitting them back out again. The funnel of the tornado seemed to dance hypnotically, like a snake waving its body to the tune of a charmer's pipe.

The camera panned round and Russell had to catch his breath. The screen showed some nearby buildings: compared with the tornado they seemed tiny. In reality, Russell could tell, they were huge. It only served to highlight just how big the twister actually was.

The screen went blank. The footage of the tornado couldn't have lasted for more than ten seconds, but it had been enough to make it clear that a major natural disaster was unfolding before his eyes.

'*For those who have just joined us,*' the news reporter's shocked voice continued, '*we are bringing you footage of the devastating storms that are battering the Florida coast and the Caribbean at this very moment. Hurricane Jasmine took weather forecasters completely by surprise and it is threatening to cause the worst natural disaster this region – no stranger to hurricanes – has yet seen.*'

'Oh, my . . .'

Russell spun round to see his wife standing behind him, her hand over her mouth. He didn't know how long she had been standing there, but she had clearly seen enough to understand what was going on. Ordinarily this would have been the moment when Bel – a vigorous environmental campaigner – would launch into a speech about global warming and the terrible effect man was having on the planet. Not today, though. Today her one concern was the same as Russell's.

'Ben,' she whispered. 'Is he . . . ?'

'I don't know,' Russell replied grimly. He strode over to the little telephone table in the corner of the room and opened the well-thumbed address book that lay there. He found Alec's number and quickly dialled it. His heart was in his throat as he waited for a reply.

But there was none. Just a friendly recorded message. *The number you have dialled is unavailable. Please try again later.*

Russell cursed. 'The phone lines must be down,' he said flatly. 'I can't get hold of Alec.'

'What about Ben's mobile.'

Russell nodded and tried the number that he knew off by heart. He simply received another recorded message: '*Hi, this is Ben. Leave me a message.*'

'Ben,' Russell said gruffly. 'It's me. Your dad. We've just heard about the storms. Call as soon as you can and let us know you're all right.'

He hung up.

'He's OK,' Bel said in a quavering voice. 'I'm sure he's OK. He's a sensible boy. He'll stay out of danger.'

Russell closed his eyes. History had proved that staying out of danger was not something Ben was particularly good at. But he put that thought from his mind. He had to.

'You're right,' he replied after a moment. 'He is a sensible lad. He *will* stay out of trouble.' He took a deep breath and fixed his wife with what he hoped was a reassuring stare. 'Of course he will,' he said.

When you're driving to your death, it's hard to drive quickly.

It was all Ben could do to keep his foot on the accelerator, and even at this slow speed it was a struggle to keep the truck on course. Ben had to keep moving, though. And he had to keep quiet. He had run out of chances. For now at least.

It was pitch black outside. There was no moon and the air was thick with rain. Danny uttered an occasional instruction, but otherwise they travelled in silence, with only the noise of the storm for company.

Beside him, Ben could sense Angelo trembling. He didn't blame him. If Ben didn't have the business of driving the truck to distract him, he'd be trembling too. He felt like a condemned man in the hour before his execution, and it was a terrifying, sickening feeling. It made his limbs heavy and his spirit weak. Thoughts of his mum and dad flashed through his brain: how would they take it? They wouldn't even know how Ben had died – they'd just assume he came to a sticky end as a result of, or after, the plane crash. They would have no way of knowing that he had fallen victim to a pointless act of revenge for something that had happened thousands of miles away. Maybe it was for the best. Maybe his death would seem less senseless that way.

These were horrible thoughts. It was all he could do to stop panic from overwhelming him; but panic, he knew from experience, wouldn't help him now. He needed a calm head and a clear mind, so that was what he concentrated on keeping.

Time had no meaning on that awful journey, so Ben couldn't have told how much later it was that his head-lamps fell upon a high wire fence and an orange and white barrier blocking the road. The fence was rattling in the wind, but so far it had held fast. There was a booth next to the barrier, but it seemed empty. He came to a halt.

'What now?' he demanded of Danny.

Their captor thought about it for a moment. 'Drive through it,' he instructed. 'Break it down.'

Ben started to argue. 'I can't just—'

'*Break it down!*' Danny insisted.

Ben found himself biting his lower lip. There was clearly nothing he could say. He gritted his teeth, revved the engine and, when it was almost screaming, let go of the handbrake. The truck shot forward, like a stone from a catapult. Angelo shouted in fright as they smashed through the barrier; a glance from Ben in the rear-view mirror showed the bits of debris flying into the air and then out of sight.

'Continue on this road,' Danny instructed. 'We're nearly there. Hurry up.'

The last thing Ben felt like doing was speeding. He simply couldn't go quickly. As they trundled down the road he occasionally had to swerve to avoid obstacles in their way, but in truth his attention was not entirely fixed on the way ahead. The headlamps of the truck had started to illuminate the outskirts of the metal city into which they were driving.

Without even wondering why he had not done so before, he scanned the dashboard for the switch that would put the headlamps onto full beam. The moment he located it, he flicked it on.

And then he gasped.

It was not the size of the structures that awaited them that astonished him; it was not the way they looked like something out of a futuristic movie; nor the way that, lit up only by the truck, the tops of the towers disappeared into the night. It was not the sheeting rain or the ominous metallic creaks caused by the wind that were so loud they could hear them above the storm.

In fact, it was nothing to do with the oil refinery that made Ben gasp.

It was the dead body, dressed only in its underwear,

that was lying by the side of the road. Ben felt his eyes glued to the sight as they drove slowly past. The body's limbs were fixed in horribly contorted positions. Ben had the feeling that it was not lying where it fell, but that the storm had blown it and rolled it towards the road. Most grisly of all was the neck. It was nothing but a gaping wound that barely connected the head to the rest of the body. Ben was no expert in these things, but whoever this was looked like they had been shot in the neck at close range.

He felt Angelo tremble even more violently beside him. 'Don't look at it,' he told his friend, and as he spoke he realized that his voice was wavering. 'Just don't look at it.' Ben dragged his own gaze away from the horrific sight of the corpse and back onto the open road ahead.

And that was when he saw the figure in the luminous green jacket.

It was standing in the middle of the road perhaps thirty metres ahead of them. As they drew closer, Ben saw that it was a man. His legs were slightly apart and he did not move, despite that fact that his hair and clothes were blowing fiercely in the strong winds and the rain was lashing down in torrents. Ben slowed the truck down as the figure showed no intention of moving out of their way.

They came to a halt only metres away from him. Ben

squinted his eyes to get a better look. The man had a few days' stubble and the hair on his head was soaked and dishevelled. He was a handsome person, however, despite the fact that he had a strangely dead look in his eyes. And despite the fact that in his right hand he carried a handgun. The moment Ben noticed the weapon, the man raised it to the windscreen. Angelo clamped his eyes shut; Ben just watched as the figure approached, keeping the gun held towards them and walking round to the driver's door.

He rapped on the window with the gun; Ben wound it down.

The man was obviously surprised to see someone as young as Ben in the driving seat. He squinted suspiciously as he peered into the cab of the truck; only when he saw that Danny was holding Ben at gunpoint and that Angelo had his arms tied did he seem to realize what was going on. His face relaxed slightly. 'Everything under control?' he shouted at Danny in a very English accent.

Danny nodded. 'Which way?' he demanded.

'Straight on. The road forks around the main central tower. Stop there – it's where we'll put him.' His eyes passed from Angelo to Ben. 'I mean *them*.'

'Are you getting in?'

The man shook his head. 'You look cosy enough. I'll travel in the back.'

With that he disappeared. Ben vaguely heard the sound of him loading himself into the back of the truck before Danny spoke. 'You heard,' their captor said quietly. 'Time to go.'

Ben just sat there.

'*Move!*' Danny instructed. His voice wavered slightly, but he prodded Ben with the gun to reinforce his point.

Ben nodded and took a deep breath. Then he started the car up again and continued trundling along the road.

It took a few minutes to get to the fork in the road that the man had indicated. As they approached it, Ben couldn't help looking, wide-eyed, at the immense tower ahead. There was no doubt that this was the one the man meant, and it was with a sickening coldness that seemed to freeze the blood in his veins that Ben let the truck come to a halt once more. Angelo looked like his body had gone limp: his head was slumped on his shoulders and his nervous breathing came in deep gulps.

'This is where we say goodbye,' Danny announced. He stared straight ahead, seemingly unwilling to look either Ben or Angelo in the eye.

'So this is it, is it, Danny?' Ben asked. 'After everything that's happened today, you're just going to leave us?'

Danny didn't reply. He didn't even give any indication he had heard what Ben said.

Ben carried on talking – suddenly the words seemed to be spilling out of him.

'I want to know something, Danny. It's something only you can tell me. Back at the wardens' station, when you knocked me out – why didn't you just *shoot* me then? It would have been much easier, wouldn't it? Much easier with me out of the way and just Angelo to deal with.'

Danny's lips curled slightly, but he still didn't answer. From the corner of his eye, Ben saw the figure of the man walking through the wind and the rain to the front of the truck. A new sense of urgency surged through him.

'You know what I think?' he almost hissed. 'I think you couldn't do it. I think you're not cut out for this, Danny. I think you're not the terrorist you're trying to be. You're blinded by your anger, but deep down you know this is wrong.'

Still no response.

'*Look at me, Danny!*' Ben urged. 'At least look me in the eye before you kill me. Because that's what you're about to do, as sure as if you pulled that trigger on me now. You leave us with that lunatic out there and you're a murderer – not just of us, but maybe of thousands of others. So at least do me the courtesy of looking at me.'

195

Slowly, as though he had to force his muscles to move, Danny turned his head. And in the dim light, Ben could see that there was doubt in his eyes. His face looked racked with indecision, and in that moment, Ben knew he had a chance.

He knew that now was the time to play his final card.

'What if she were here, Danny?' he asked, his voice low and intense. 'What if Basheera were here now? What if she knew what you were doing? What would she say to you?'

Danny seemed to freeze. 'What do you mean?' he asked, his voice strangled.

'You know what I mean,' Ben replied. At the front of the car the man was standing in the wind and the rain, waving his handgun in their direction to indicate that they should get out of the car. '*You know what I mean, Danny.* She would tell you that this isn't the way. She would tell you to listen to me, to listen to Angelo. He can speak to his father. He can get the oil men to leave your island.' He narrowed his eyes. 'If you do this, Danny, the only thing your sister will be remembered for is the death of other people.'

'*Shut up!*' Danny screamed suddenly and so violently that it made Ben jump. '*You don't know what you're talking about. Just shut up and get out of the truck!*' His face was filled with rage; his hands were shaking. For a terrifying moment Ben thought he was going to fire the gun; instead he nudged it sharply into his ribs, winding him and forcing him to catch his breath.

At that very moment the door opened. Ben's ears were filled with the sudden rush of the wind and the rain sheeted ferociously into the cab of the truck. He felt himself being pulled out of the pick-up by the scruff of his neck. While Danny had been screaming at him, the man outside had clearly had enough of waiting. He pulled Ben roughly from the truck and then, with a sharp crack, whacked him across the side of the head with the handle of his gun. Blood flowed into Ben's eyes, blinding him momentarily. He was pushed to the floor and then kicked harshly in the stomach.

His body curled up into a protective ball and he looked up. The man was staring down at him with a severe, uncompromising look on his face. He looked deeply sinister with his hair blowing in the wind and backed by the thick, unrelenting rain; and as Ben lay there in agony, one thing became very, very clear to him.

He might suspect Danny of having doubts; but this new stranger had none whatsoever. He was here to do a job, and he wouldn't be leaving until it was fully accomplished.

Chapter Sixteen

The next thing Ben knew he was being pulled to his feet again, before Angelo was dragged unceremoniously out of the pick-up.

'I'll take it from here,' the new man barked at Danny. 'If you want my advice, put some distance between yourself and the refinery. Several miles. When it blows, it's *really* going to blow.'

Danny didn't reply. He seemed uncomfortable as he moved into the driving seat.

'You should head south, down to the Keys. The storm's moving north so things should be less dangerous there.'

Danny made no sign that he was even listening. He just breathed deeply and stared straight ahead. The man shrugged. 'It's up to you,' he shouted. He looked at his watch. 'You've got an hour before I detonate. Maybe a few minutes longer.' He slammed the door shut.

The thought of being left with this man made all the strength sap from Ben's body. It took a superhuman effort to summon up the energy to throw himself towards the pick-up and bang his fist against Danny's window. He shouted out at him one last time. '*Think of Basheera, Danny!*' he yelled. '*Think of what she'd say! Think of—*'

He never finished his sentence, because the man thumped him on the side of the face for a second time. It sent an agonizing, stinging pain down one side of his body and he felt dizzy. He fell to the floor again. The man started shouting. 'Get to your feet!' he bellowed.

Ben could barely move; but just then he felt the unmistakable clunk of cold steel against his head. 'I said, get to your feet. You've got five seconds.' The man was having to scream over the wind and the rain.

Ben groaned as he forced himself to stand up. As he did, he watched, with a horrible sinking feeling, as the pick-up truck started to move. Danny reversed in a semi-circle so that the vehicle was pointing back the way they had come. He came to a brief halt and stared at them through the window. Ben stared back, jutting out his chin defiantly and trying to ignore the pain from the bleeding wound on his face. Danny's expression hardened. He nodded to himself, and then drove off.

Ben watched the pick-up truck trundle away, its rear lights becoming blurred and hazy from the rain. He wasn't allowed to wait until they disappeared, however. Their new captor clearly had plans for them. And he was obviously in a hurry.

'Move,' the man told them. He rapped Ben on the back of the head with his gun to underline his command. Ben's eyes flickered to his right. Angelo was there, his hands still tied behind his back and his head bowed. He looked exhausted and dejected, as if he wasn't even aware of the howling gales and pounding rain around them. Just then there was an ominous creek. It was the sort of noise Ben was used to hearing at home in the middle of the night, only this was a hundred times louder. It sounded like the huge tower ahead of them was being forced from its roots, as though it was about to split in two and empty its oily guts all over them at any moment.

'*Move!*' the man repeated. He pushed Angelo, who stumbled forward. Ben instinctively grabbed his friend's arm to stop him from falling, then looked back at the man behind them, the rain almost blinding him.

'Where?' he demanded.

The man used his gun to reply, pointing it towards the tower. Ben's face set into an expression of grim concentration and, still holding Angelo's arm, he walked in that direction.

The cold rain and the wind didn't even affect him now. He hardly noticed them. His mind was on other things: on Danny, and the way he had betrayed them; on his own stupidity for not listening to Brad the body-guard and being suspicious of absolutely *everyone* on that plane. He tried his best not to think about what was awaiting them, because every time he did that, he felt horribly sick.

It took them less than a minute to reach the foot of the tower. It stretched above them into the darkness like a giant, and the creaking sound – like the giant's roars – now dwarfed even the sound of the storm.

'Stop!' the man shouted from behind them.

They did as they were told and Ben turned to look at him again.

He was skirting round them, his gun still firmly pointed in their direction. The man edged towards the door of a low building that was situated below the tower. Ben couldn't really make out what it looked like from this distance – it was too dark, and the rain hampered his vision. He could see what the man was doing, however. He tried the door: it was locked. He banged against it with his foot as though he might be able to force it open with a good kick, but it only made a dull, metallic echo. And so he stood back, a good two metres, and pointed his gun towards the door.

Now's your chance, Ben urged himself. If he could

rush the guy while his gun was pointing in a different direction . . .

Too late. The man fired at the lock of the door. The crack of the gun seemed to echo all around the refinery like a sudden crack of thunder. The bullet sparked against the door and there was a second, less obvious bang as it ricocheted off. It had done its work well, however. The door shuddered from the impact and then slowly, as if being opened by some sinister and unseen butler, swung open.

Without hesitation, the man strode back towards them. He grabbed Angelo's free arm and pushed him in the direction of the building. Ben followed. As he did so, he felt the man's gun against the back of his head once more. It was warm this time. Warm from use. It was the sort of warmth that made Ben shudder.

They were hustled through the open door and into the building where, for a moment, they stood in darkness. Ben felt the water dripping from his clothes as he heard the man clattering around. Suddenly he squinted as the lights were switched on – two flickering strip bulbs on the ceiling that flooded the room with a harsh, unnatural brightness. It took several seconds for him to be able to open his eyes properly: when he did, he looked around to get his bearings.

They were in some sort of control room. Along the far wall, opposite the open door, there was a bank of instruments, dials and levers. There were also a couple of computer screens with keyboards, but these were switched off, and some swivel chairs. The chairs were not pushed neatly against the control panel, but instead were dotted around messily. It looked like whoever had last been in this room had left in a hurry. There were no windows; instead the walls were covered with complicated charts and measurements, which would have made Ben glaze over a bit even if he felt like looking at them.

He didn't feel like looking at them, though. And he didn't have the time, because at that precise moment he felt a sharp blow just behind his knees. His legs collapsed beneath him and he fell with a heavy thud to the ground. He was joined moments later by Angelo, who had just received the same treatment and who called out in pain as his knees cracked against the hard floor.

Their dripping wet clothes had already made a small puddle around them and briefly Ben caught sight of his own reflection in it. He looked terrible: exhausted and scared. *Hardly surprising*, he thought to himself. His reflection disappeared as the puddle wavered slightly. A rope suddenly appeared in front of him and he gasped as he felt it being tied tightly around his waist, then coiled several times more, despite the fact that he had started to struggle violently. The man behind him was breathing heavily as he gripped the rope firmly; he grunted with satisfaction when Ben had to catch his own breath as the rope was tightly tied. Ben's arms were immobile – there was no way he was going to get out of that.

Despite the fact that Angelo already had his arms tied behind his back he received the same treatment.

'Get to your feet,' the man instructed. Ben struggled up painfully, as did Angelo.

The man walked towards the control panel. 'Over here,' he said. The two boys followed him. Ben watched as he took the end of the rope that bound Angelo and tied it to the sturdy metal leg of the control bench. He then pushed Ben to the other end of the bench and tied him to another leg. He and Angelo were out of reach of each other and Ben could tell that he'd have had enough trouble untying the fiendish knots the man had made even if his hands were free; now they were tied behind his back, he'd have no chance.

The man took his rucksack from his back, placed it on the floor and bent down to get something from inside. 'What are you doing?' Ben asked, his nervous voice croaking; but the man didn't answer. Instead he pulled what looked like a small video camera from the bag and started tinkering with it. When he was satisfied that it was working, he turned to Angelo.

'I'm going to film you,' he said curtly. 'When I nod, you say your name for the camera, and that you are currently at the South Miami Oil Refinery.'

Angelo raised his bowed head and fixed the man with a look of hate. He curled his lip. 'And if I don't?' he demanded.

The man's eyes narrowed. He let the camera fall to his side, then approached Angelo with the gun. He held it to the Italian boy's head.

'You may be under the mistaken impression,' he whispered, 'that I'm the kind of person who likes to be messed with. That's not a mistake people make more than once. Understand?'

Terrified and trembling, Angelo nodded his head.

'Good,' the man continued. 'Now listen carefully. I'm not a very patient film director, so you only get one shot at this. No retakes.'

He stepped back a few paces, raised the camera again and pressed a button. A little red light appeared at the front as the man nodded at Angelo.

The Italian boy tried to speak, but his voice failed him at first. When he finally did manage to get the words out, they were weak and wavering. 'My name . . .' he stuttered. 'My name is Angelo Bandini.' He took a deep, trembling breath. 'I am in the middle of the South Miami Oil Refinery.' He stared, white-faced at the camera. 'Please don't kill me,' he begged quietly. '*Please don't kill me . . .*'

But the man had already stopped recording and was stashing the camera back in his rucksack. Once it was stowed away, he turned his back on the two of them and made to leave. He strode towards the door and was just about to walk out when Ben shouted.

'Wait!'

The man stopped in his tracks. He paused, as though deciding whether to answer Ben's call or not, then slowly turned. He had one eyebrow raised, and he stared at Ben with a dead look in his face.

'What?'

Ben looked at him urgently. 'Think about what you're doing. Think about what it's going to mean. This isn't going to help the people on Danny's island – it's not going to do them any good at all!'

The man blinked at him, expressionlessly. Then his lip curled and he let out a small snort of laughter. '*Help* them?' he demanded in his upper-class English accent. He looked back over his shoulder. 'Help *him*? You think I'm doing this because I want to help the inhabitants of some godforsaken place thousands of miles away? You must be stupider than you look.'

Ben ignored the insult. The lights flickered off and on again.

'Then why?' he whispered. 'Why are you doing this?'

The man smirked, then walked up to him. He put his face only inches from Ben's and spoke in a slow, clear voice. He sounded patronizing, as though he was explaining something to a particularly idiotic child. 'For money,' he rasped. 'I'm being very well paid. Now if you'll excuse me, I've a little more work to do.'

He stepped back and headed for the door once more.

'If it's money you want,' Angelo shouted at him, 'I can pay you. I'm rich. Just name your price.'

The man turned round and his eyes widened. 'Really?' he asked, his voice dripping with sarcasm. 'And I suppose you wouldn't even think about going back on your word once you're safely in Daddy's arms, would you?' He sneered. 'Don't be so stupid.'

'Stupid?' Ben demanded angrily. 'Who's the stupid one? How many people do you think you're about to kill?' Now the man looked annoyed, but Ben didn't care. 'There's me and Angelo,' he pressed. 'That's two. But then there's everyone else who'll die when the wind spreads the flames and the smoke. How much are their lives worth to you?'

The man didn't answer. Instead, he raised his gun and pointed it directly at Ben. 'You're a noisy kid,' he announced. 'Maybe I should just silence you right now.'

The threat hung between them for a few long seconds. Ben jutted out his chin defiantly. If this was the end, he wasn't going to give the man the satisfaction of having him beg for mercy.

Then, gradually, the man lowered the gun.

'No,' he whispered. 'I don't think so. I've gone to a lot of trouble to arrange this evening's little spectacular. It would be a dreadful shame if you weren't around to witness the fireworks.' He looked at his watch. 'Showtime,' he said, 'in about an hour. Unfortunately I won't be able to watch it as I have a prior appointment elsewhere – once I've found myself a decent vehicle in which to get out of here. But don't worry – the little remote detonator in my bag has a very long range. I'm sure everything will go with a bang.'

He furrowed his brow a little before continuing to speak, this time in a far less sarcastic voice. 'I really don't know who you are,' he addressed Ben directly, 'or how you got involved in all this. But you seem like the kind of lad who's happy to poke his nose into other people's business. Nobody likes a nosy kid, so I don't suppose you'll be terribly mourned.'

Ben looked at him defiantly. 'I've just been trying to help my friend,' he retorted. 'I don't suppose it's some- thing you'd understand.'

A look of mock surprise crossed the man's face. 'A friend?' He sneered. 'Oh, how sweet.'

And with that, he turned for the final time. He switched off the light to the control room, plunging

Ben and Angelo into darkness, before closing the door ominously behind him.

Think of Basheera, Danny! Think of what she'd say!

Ben's words echoed in Danny's head. He tried to get rid of that silent sound, but he couldn't. In a burst of anger he thumped his fist against the steering wheel as he tried to empty his mind.

Even with the weather, everything important was going according to plan. Why, then, did Danny feel so empty?

The lashing of the wind and the rain against the pick-up truck had taken him by surprise. It was difficult to manoeuvre the vehicle. Very difficult. Young Ben had done well. He was a strong boy. Brave too. The things he had done that day would have been hard for almost anyone, even if they'd had the guts to do them. Danny regretted having to leave Ben at the oil refinery. He regretted it deeply.

The pick-up truck trundled away from the centre of the refinery. The headlamps illuminated the sheeting rain and then, by the side of the road, the dead body of the refinery worker that they had seen on the way in. It looked just as gruesome now as it had then. More so, perhaps. Danny averted his eyes. He was not used to the sight of death. Strange, then, that he had woken up that morning expecting the day to bring his own death, as well as that of many others.

In his mind it had seemed noble and glorious. It had seemed like he was striking a blow for the oppressed. It seemed like the right thing to do. But now, as he crept away through the dreadful storms, leaving Ben and Angelo at the hands of the mercenary who was being paid a great deal of money to carry out the wishes of his people, he felt far from noble. Far from glorious. He felt like a sneak.

'Shut up,' he whispered to himself in his own language. These were harmful thoughts, creeping into his brain like the roots of a poisonous plant. He was being distracted from what he had set out to do that morning: to avenge his sister and bring the plight of his people to the attention of the world. He glanced left and right at the huge construction of pipes and machinery that surrounded him like the intestines of some great metal beast. When it exploded, it would be like a beacon, appearing on the television screens of people around the world and making them realize that the oil men could not continue to behave as they had been doing. That it would not be tolerated. And if Ben and Angelo had to be sacrificed to make that point, so be it . . .

Ben and Angelo.

As Danny approached the exit of the refinery, a picture filled his mind. It was of the two boys, tied up and frightened in the moments before the explosion.

The image needled his confused mind and he thought of Ben's accusation: that Danny could not shoot him in cold blood. That he didn't have the stomach for it. That by doing things this way, he was pretending that he was not a murderer. Somewhere, deep inside, a little voice was telling him that this was true.

Think of Basheera, Danny! Think of what she'd say!

What would she say? Would she thank him for this? Would she even understand what was happening? His little sister was only nine years old when she died, but there was something in those big eyes of hers that made her seem older. Made her seem like she *understood*. Would she realize that her brother's actions – that the actions of everyone in their village – were on her account?

Would she let it happen?

Danny's lips narrowed. He was out of the refinery now, back on the main road. He should speed up. Get away from there as quickly as possible. But something was stopping him, and it wasn't just the storm. He drew a deep breath, then thumped the steering wheel again. The horn sounded, but there was no one there to hear it.

You must keep driving, he told himself. It is your duty to keep driving. Your duty to the village. Your duty to your grieving mother and father. Your duty to yourself. And most of all, your duty to Basheera.

Basheera.

He pictured her. She was such a happy little girl. So full of fun and full of love for everyone. He pictured her sitting there next to him, in the place where Angelo had sat with his hands tied behind his back. And in his mind she began to speak.

'*It is not their fault, my brother*,' she said softly, her childlike voice firm but kind. '*I do not want them to come to harm.*'

Danny blinked. Basheera's voice had been quite clear, as though she really were sitting there next to him. Or at least her ghost.

He shook his head. It was the storm. The wind shrieking. It was making him uneasy, now that he was all alone. His mind was playing tricks on him. He pressed down on the accelerator.

The wind howled again, and with it came Basheera's voice once more.

'*And what of the others?*' she asked lightly. '*The others who will die.*'

Danny's head shot round. There was only an empty seat next to him, but it had sounded for all the world like Basheera was there. As he took his eyes off the road, the car veered and he was forced to slam the brakes down and come to a screeching halt. He sat there for a moment, panting and sweating, as the wind outside continued to sing to him.

How like the wailing of a human voice it sounded. It was as though the very earth was lamenting what was about to happen.

Suddenly he could take it no more. Hardly knowing what he was doing, he opened the door of the car and jumped out. The rain stung him as it pelted into his face, and the door – blowing in the wind – almost knocked him over. But he kept his footing and looked up to the sky.

He shouted in a loud voice. A voice that made him hoarse. Had anyone been there on that deserted road to hear him, they would not have heard what he said above the wind. But it was a loud voice nevertheless.

'*Do not lecture me!*' he screamed in his own language. '*Do not lecture me, and do not disapprove! Do you think I woke this morning prepared to give my life lightly? This is for you, Basheera. Understand that. This is for you.*'

Chapter Seventeen

Ben sat in the darkness. His muscles were frozen – not with cold, but with fear.

It was pitch black. There wasn't even a glimmer of light, so his night vision failed to alleviate the darkness. Inside the control room, the two of them were silent; but there was noise all around. The wind, for a start – it howled and shrieked like some demented banshee. The rain hammered down on the roof of the building. Ben hadn't seen what it was made of, but it sounded like corrugated iron – the water echoed as it hit, resonating like an immense drum. The noise of the rain came in fits and starts: loud first, then soft, then loud again. Ben pictured it being blown in erratic swirls by the wind.

And above everything else – above the dreadful sounds of the storm – there was the creaking of the refinery around them. It was as if the whole area was groaning from the battering of the elements. And it sounded like it was at breaking point. No wonder the place had been deserted, Ben thought to himself. Only a fool would stay here in these conditions.

'He's going to do it, isn't he?' Angelo interrupted Ben's morose thoughts. 'He's actually going to do it.' The Italian's voice was hushed, barely audible above the noise outside.

'Yeah,' Ben replied solemnly. 'Yeah, I think he is.'

A pause.

'You know what the stupid thing is?' Angelo asked.

'No. What?'

'I actually agree with Danny. I hate my dad's business. It's so . . .' He searched for the word. '*Greedy*.'

Above them there was a sudden groan. Ben held his breath – it sounded like something was on the brink of collapsing. After a few seconds, though, it stopped, to be replaced once more by the sound of the hurricane.

'How long do you think we've got?' Angelo asked.

Ben thought about it. In the darkness, time meant very little. It could have been five minutes since the man had left them here; it could have been half an hour. On balance, he thought time had probably been passing slowly. 'I reckon we've been here about ten minutes. He said an hour, so . . .'

'So we've got fifty minutes to live,' Angelo stated dramatically.

His words had an immediate effect on Ben. He was suddenly filled with rage, with an absolute determination to get out of here. He stood up and started to pull at the rope with the full weight of his body. It did nothing, and he cursed.

'*Cosa fai?*' Angelo asked, clearly alerted by the sound of Ben moving. 'What are you doing?'

'Get up,' Ben said. 'Walk towards me. If we can get close enough, maybe we can undo each other.' Deep down he knew they *weren't* close enough. But they were desperate and anything was worth a try.

There was a scuffling sound as Angelo hurried to his feet. 'Where are you?' he asked.

'Here,' Ben announced as he stepped blindly in Angelo's direction. It only took a few paces, however, before he felt the pull of the rope and was unable to walk any further.

'It's no good,' Angelo announced. 'We're too far apart.'

Ben had to concede that it was true. 'There must be some way out,' he raged. 'There must be *something* we can do.' Backing up in the direction of the control bench, he groped in the dark as well as his bound hands could manage, hoping to find something sharp against which to slice the rope. But there was nothing.

Elsewhere in the room he could sense Angelo beginning to panic.

'It's no good,' the Italian wailed. 'We're going to die.' A brief moment of silence, and then: 'Do you think it will hurt, Ben? When the factory explodes, I mean. Do you think we will feel it?'

Ben felt the muscles in his face set into an expression of determination. 'We're not going to die,' he said from behind gritted teeth. 'We're going to get out of here somehow.' He tugged sharply at the rope yet again, but still nothing happened.

Angelo's voice became angry. 'What do you mean, we're going to get out of here? It's useless, Ben. Can't you see that? We've been lucky so far today, but this is it. *There's nothing we can do!* We might as well just sit here and wait for it to happen.'

And it was at just that moment that Ben's eyes were blinded.

He screwed his eyes closed and bowed his head as the pain of the sudden bright light subsided. Then, gingerly, he looked back towards where the light had come from. The door was open and standing there, illuminated from behind by the bright beams of a vehicle's headlamps, was a figure. For several seconds it did not move – it just stood there, a dark silhouette – and Ben felt a curious mixture of relief and fear. Then it stepped to one side, disappearing from Ben's vision.

'Help us!' Ben called. 'We're tied up. You have to . . .'

He stopped as the main lights flickered on.

It took a few seconds for his eyes to get used to the brightness, and a few more to make out the features of the man standing there.

He had tanned skin and dark hair that was dishevelled from being out in the wind and the rain. His clothes were soaked and he had an urgent, uncertain look in his brown eyes. He was looking not at Ben, but at Angelo, and he was breathing heavily.

'*Danny*,' the two of them whispered in unison.

Danny stood there, as though lost for words.

'Danny,' Ben urged. He felt like he was on the edge of a precipice – any minute now he could fall to his death. 'You've *got* to untie us. This place could blow any minute.'

Danny barely blinked.

'*You've got to help us, Danny.*' As he spoke, Ben struggled to free himself from the ropes, but of course it was useless.

Danny took three uncertain steps towards Angelo. When he finally spoke, his voice was strangled.

'You said you can speak to your father?' he asked.

Angelo nodded mutely.

'And what will you tell him?'

The Italian boy blinked and Ben held his breath. It was all up to Angelo now; all up to his dishevelled friend who only a second ago had been wailing with panic. Ben willed him to say the right thing – whatever that was.

'I will tell him,' Angelo replied, 'what has happened to me. I will tell him that I nearly died. And I will tell him that it is his fault and that if he does not stop doing the things that he is doing, he is no longer my father and I am no longer his son.'

Angelo stared at Danny, a wide-eyed, open stare that made it clear he meant what he said. Danny returned that gaze with a look that expressed a world of doubt and indecision.

And then he stepped forward.

'Turn round,' he told Angelo.

The Italian boy did as he was told. Ben watched as Danny started to untie the knot that bound him. Within seconds Angelo was uncoiling himself and Danny was working on Ben's ropes. 'We've got to stop this happening,' Ben said before he was even free. 'Danny, do you know where the bomb is? He said he had a detonator, but if we can get the explosives away from the refinery . . .'

He was untied now, so he spun round to uncoil himself.

Danny was ashen-faced and Ben noticed that his hands were shaking. 'I'm sorry,' Danny started to say. 'You tried to stop me, but I wouldn't listen . . .'

Ben took a deep breath, stepped over to Danny and held him by the shoulders. 'Forget about it,' he told the man sincerely. 'It's water under the bridge and we've got other things to concentrate on. The explosives, Danny. Do you know where they are?'

Danny shook his head. 'All I know,' he replied, 'is that there's more than one of them.'

'More than one? How many?'

'I don't know.' As he spoke, the tower above them creaked ominously once more.

'We need to get out of here, Ben,' Angelo said urgently. He was already halfway to the door.

Ben felt as if untying the rope had freed his mind as well as his body. All the possible scenarios seemed to be flashing through his head. 'We don't know how much time we've got,' he announced quickly. 'This place is massive – without knowing where the devices are, we'll never find them in time.' He looked at the others. 'Get to the truck!' he yelled. 'The mercenary said he had a remote detonator. The only way we can stop the refinery from blowing is by catching up with him and getting hold of the detonator.'

They were all moving towards the door now, but Angelo looked at Ben as if he was mad. 'But we don't know where he is!' he shouted.

'Yes we do,' Ben yelled as they ran outside into the rain.

Angelo looked at him in confusion. 'Where?'

'The Keys. He told Danny to head for the Keys, remember? The Florida Keys – it's a series of long, thin islands to the south of here.'

'Ben's right,' Danny barked. 'He'll definitely be heading south. We need to hurry.'

Instinctively, Ben ran round to the driver's side of the car; as he did so, he heard Danny shouting.

'No, Ben,' he yelled. 'I need to drive.'

'Why?'

'Think about it. If we catch up with him, we'll need to get him to stop. He'll only do that if he thinks it's just me in the truck.'

Ben narrowed his eyes slightly. He still didn't quite trust Danny, but he had to agree that he was right: the mercenary wasn't simply going to pull over just because Ben and Angelo were asking him nicely. He looked at the back of the pick-up. It was swimming with water and the rear guard was rattling ominously in the wind. It didn't look like the most luxurious way to travel. In fact, it would be positively dangerous – exposed to the elements they would be at risk from the flying debris and whatever else the storm hurled at them.

'We could travel in the front and just keep our heads down,' Angelo suggested.

Ben thought about it. 'No,' he decided finally. 'I don't think so. If the pick-up comes to a stop, we need to be properly out of sight. The back of the truck's the only real option.'

Angelo didn't argue. Together they climbed up into the rear of the pick-up. Their clothes were wet already, so it didn't matter that they found themselves sitting in cold water; but it still promised to be a bruising, uncomfortable ride.

'I'll go as fast as I can,' Danny shouted at them. 'If we're going to catch up with him I need to put my foot down. You'll have to hold on tightly.'

Ben looked around. There really didn't seem to be much they *could* hold onto.

'Do you know what he's driving?' Angelo asked.

Danny shook his head. 'The roads are clear, though. We'll just have to hope we can stop him.'

Suddenly a memory popped into Ben's head. He looked at Angelo. 'Just before he left us, do you remember him saying something about having to get hold of a vehicle?'

Angelo winced. 'I was a bit distracted . . .'

'He did,' Ben shouted. 'Danny, look for a big truck, like the ones we've seen here. That's what he'll be driving – I'm sure of it.'

Danny nodded and without another word disappeared into the front of the truck. The engine spluttered slightly, then started turning over. They moved off.

Ben could tell that Danny was having the same trouble he himself had encountered in keeping the vehicle straight in the wind. Their bodies banged painfully against the hard metal sides of the pick-up as the vehicle rocked from side to side and Ben found himself slipping and sliding on the wet surface. He clutched onto the edge of the truck. If they approached the mercenary, they'd have to duck down, but for now this would be OK. He saw that Angelo was doing the same thing, and the wind screamed in their ears as they clung grimly to the side of the truck.

Ben tried not to look at the dead body as they approached it again, but somehow he found his eyes glued to that grisly sight. As they passed, he wondered who the dead man was. Did he have a family? Children? Had he come to work that morning thinking that today would be just another day? He noticed that Angelo could not take his eyes off the dead man either. Surely his Italian friend's feelings were even more complicated than Ben's. This was his father's refinery; his father's workforce. The man lying dead on the ground had even less reason to be killed than Angelo. It was an uncomfortable thought.

Five people in Ben's immediate vicinity had died that day: the two pilots, the bodyguard, the hijacker and this guy. The body count was mounting and it was not lost on Ben that he and the other two people in the truck were the only ones who could stop it from getting any worse. He fixed that thought in his mind as the corpse disappeared into the distance.

The fence at the boundary of the oil refinery, which had held up to the winds when they arrived, was now flattened, and the remains of the barrier that Ben had smashed through had long since blown away in the wind. It was an alarming sight, of course, but somehow Ben felt a bit better crossing over the boundary of the refinery. If it blew up any time soon, they'd be dead in seconds, but at least they were getting away. He took a deep breath and looked out into the distance.

It all happened in a few seconds. The sky almost appeared to part – in truth it was just a momentary clearing of the cloud cover. The moon, bright and full, appeared. It lit them up brightly and Ben was half aware of its reflection on the water that had collected in the back of the truck. He blinked, then stared as the whole sky seemed suddenly to be illuminated. After the darkness and the rain it was an extraordinary sight. Like the sun coming up.

But it was not the moon itself that commanded Ben's attention.

It was something else.

It was impossible to tell how close it was or even, in the first instant, *what* it was. It towered in the distance: a great black funnel with a bulbous, mushroom-like top. How high up into the sky it reached, Ben could never have said, but it seemed to reach halfway up to heaven. It sent a chill through his blood, and yet he was transfixed by it: transfixed by the way it seemed to shimmy, snake-like, from side to side; transfixed by the absolute enormity and absolute terror of it; transfixed by the way it seemed to be moving at once infinitely slowly and impossibly quickly, a colossus of pent-up power, heading straight for them, ready to strike.

The very sight made his breath catch in his throat and he felt, for one horrible moment, as though he would be sick with fear.

'*What is it?*' he heard Angelo scream.

Ben couldn't take his eyes away from that awesome sight. Then, as quickly as it had appeared, the moon retreated behind some fast-scudding clouds and Ben's vision was obscured once more. He turned to look at Angelo and uttered a single word.

'Tornado.'

And then, because he realized he had barely whispered it and that Angelo could never have heard what he said, he repeated himself.

'*Tornado!*'

The two friends looked at each other in horror. The words they had heard on the radio were ringing in Ben's ears: *Hurricane Jasmine has spawned a severe tornado, category F3, currently approaching the south-eastern*

Florida area. It is fast-moving and extremely destructive.
He had no idea what category F3 meant, but if what he
had just seen was anything to go by, it meant something
bad. The twister looked as if it could eat up the oil
refinery and spew it out in seconds. Just imagine, he
thought to himself, what it could do if the place were
on fire . . .

He shook his head as though waking from a dream.
Up until then he had forgotten all about the tornado.
Not any more, though. The thing he had just seen was
huge.

Terrifyingly huge.

He closed his eyes and pictured the geography of
Florida. The Keys were to the south-east – exactly the
direction in which the tornado was heading. The
hurricane might be moving north, but now they had
something different to contend with. Something
bigger. Something more destructive.

Ben could hardly believe it was possible, but from
what he had just seen, his day was about to get even
worse.

Chapter Eighteen

The storm had thrown problems in his way, there had been no doubt about that. But it had made certain things easier too.

The fact that the refinery had been deserted, for instance, had been a definite advantage. No creeping around, no having to stay hidden, fewer bullets in fewer skulls. It wasn't that he minded killing people, but it definitely attracted attention and that would only have made things harder. And according to his original plan, depending on whether or not Danny had turned up with the boy, he would have had to wait until he had skulked out of the boundary of the refinery before carjacking a vehicle. It would have meant the police would have been on the lookout for him, of course, but that wouldn't have mattered. By the time the refinery had gone bang, they would have had bigger fish to fry than the problem of a stolen car.

The storms, however, had meant that he could take his pick of the vehicles inside the actual refinery. OK, they weren't likely to be zippy little sports cars but that didn't matter. As long as they got him away from the area, he was happy.

He had left the kids in the control room about five minutes ago and frankly he had been glad to see the back of them. Mouthy little fools. Arrogant. Stupid. Thinking they could stop him from doing his job with their silly little arguments and their pathetic pleas. The world would be a better place without them, he thought to himself as he scanned the surrounding area for something to drive.

It wasn't long before his eyes fell upon a suitable vehicle. It was an articulated lorry without its load – just the cab and nothing behind it. He nodded briefly to himself and then hurried through the rain to the driver's door. It felt good to climb inside out of the elements, even though his clothes were still sopping wet and he was chilled to the bone. He ignored all that, though. He carefully placed his bag on the passenger seat, then leaned to one side and ripped off the plastic plating that covered the area under the steering wheel. It only took him a minute or so to locate the two wires he needed to hotwire the truck, and seconds later the engine was turning over.

He nodded with satisfaction, then drove towards the exit.

It was difficult to keep the truck steady on account of the wind, so he drove with care. There was no hurry, after all. Nobody would be taking a sightseeing tour of the refinery just now, so there was no risk that the kids would be rescued. All he had to do was get to a safe distance – out of the way of the refinery and the course of the storms – and then detonate. Deliver the video-tape to the newspapers in a day or so and the money would be his.

He left the refinery with a pleasing sense of confidence. Everything was going like clockwork.

There was nothing quite so satisfying as a good day's work.

Danny wasn't wasting any time – Ben thought the pick-up was travelling much more quickly than when he himself was driving it. Maybe it just seemed that way: he and Angelo were being thrown around in the back with every sideways movement of the vehicle; and there were plenty of those. His body had taken some serious punishment today; now, though, he felt that it was being bruised beyond recognition.

Still, he wasn't about to complain. They had plenty of reasons to move quickly after all. It was essential that they caught up with the mercenary. The only thing that stood between them and the refinery going up in smoke was a tiny remote detonator. As they drove, nightmare flashes shrieked through Ben's mind of the man silently flicking the small switch that would cause untold disaster; when that happened, he found himself urging Danny to speed faster through the storm.

They had to stop him.

They *had* to.

But they had more than one reason for urging Danny on. The tornado – that massive, ugly giant that had flashed into their vision for only a few seconds – was following them. They couldn't see it; they couldn't even hear it above the rest of the storm. But it was there, like a stranger in the night creeping after them with a murderous intent. The very thought of it made Ben shudder and grip onto the edge of the pick-up truck that little bit more tightly.

He looked over at Angelo. His Italian friend was also hugging the edge of the truck, his long, dark hair blowing wildly in the screaming wind. Despite the terrifying scenario, however, Ben thought he could see a change in him. For the last few hours, he had seemed like all the fight had left him. He had seemed broken. But now there was a new determination about him. He had his head leaning over the edge of the pick-up truck and he was looking forward, not back.

They drove for a good twenty minutes without

seeing another moving vehicle. As they wavered down the road, Ben suddenly panicked. What if they were heading in the wrong direction? What if the mercenary wasn't driving south at all? He tried to put that thought from his mind. He had to be. He wasn't stupid enough to follow the direction of the hurricane, was he? Not that it could be worse anywhere else than it was here. Along the sides of the road were signs of the devastation the storm had caused. Cars were upturned and roofs were flapping in the wind. There were no lights on any-where, nor any sign of people. Ben wondered how long it would take to clear up this destruction. Months, probably. Years.

'*There's something up ahead!*' Angelo cried, his voice hoarse as it battled with the noise of the engine and the wind. '*I can see its lights.*'

Ben stretched his neck over the edge of the truck and looked forwards. Sure enough, in the distance he saw some lights. He couldn't tell how far away they were – the rain meant that distances were a bit hazy – but he reckoned it couldn't have been more than a couple of hundred metres.

'Get down!' he shouted at Angelo. 'We can't let him know we're here.'

Angelo nodded and the two of them flung them-selves down into the water that was sluicing around the back of the truck. It was deeply uncomfortable. With nothing to hold onto, they slid around uncontrollably. Ben felt the engine accelerating and as a result they were pushed further to the back: clearly Danny had also seen the vehicle up ahead and was risking the dangers of travelling even faster in the high winds to catch up with it.

Suddenly the truck slowed down.

Ben wished he could peer out to see what was happening but that was out of the question. Instead he stayed well hidden. Angelo was looking at him intently. 'Ready?' the Italian called grimly.

'Ready,' Ben replied. His skin was tingling with anticipation of what was to come.

The pick-up truck ground to a halt.

Ben tried to imagine what would be happening. He pictured the pick-up truck driving alongside the other vehicle, whatever it was; he imagined Danny leaning out of the window and flagging the attention of the mercenary. Now the two of them had stopped.

A car door slammed. Then another one.

Both men would be approaching each other.

Ben held his breath. It was all in Danny's hands now. All in the hands of a man Ben still couldn't be sure whether he could trust. A man who had already double-crossed them once that day. And there was nothing he or Angelo could do but wait and see what happened.

* * *

The mercenary had been keeping his eye on the road and his hands on the steering wheel. It was a difficult drive with the wind buffeting the truck from all sides, but he was in no hurry. He could afford to take it easy. To stay safe. He maintained a slow but steady speed as he continued down US Route 1. It wouldn't be long before he approached the Overseas Highway, a long road bridge that jutted up through the ocean and carried Route 1 from the Florida mainland to the Keys. He would use it to cross to Key Largo, the largest of the Keys and the nearest to the mainland. Once he was there, he estimated, he would be far enough away from the refinery and any damage the explosion might cause.

That was when he would detonate.

The roads were satisfyingly deserted. He hadn't seen a single car since he left the refinery. The evacuation process must have been swift; those that were still left would have battened down the hatches and prayed that the storm didn't cause them or their property too much damage. It suited him. It meant he had the road to himself.

Or did he?

He blinked as he looked in the rear-view mirror. Behind him, through the thick rain, he saw the un-mistakable glare of a set of headlights.

He shrugged. It didn't matter. If somebody was fool enough to be out on the roads in this weather without good reason, that was their business, not his. He directed his attention back to the road ahead and concentrated on keeping the truck steady.

It was a minute or so later that he noticed the headlamps again. This time they were much closer. He furrowed his brows. Whoever was driving the vehicle must be going very quickly. Another look in the mirror verified this: the headlamps seemed to waver from side to side. The driver was obviously having difficulty keeping the truck on the road. In response, the mercenary slowed down. He didn't want to come off worse in a collision if the idiot behind him couldn't control his vehicle. Better to let it pass than try and outrun it.

His attention was split now, half of it on the road ahead, half of it on the approaching vehicle. It was close now – blindingly close. He could not look for too long at the headlamps in the mirror for fear of dazzling himself. He cursed the driver's stupidity. He was too close. Carry on like this and it could end badly for both of them.

Suddenly the vehicle pulled out as if to overtake, then drew alongside him. It was a pick-up truck with an open back, he saw. It looked vaguely familiar, but then there were thousands of pick-up trucks across America. He slowed slightly to allow it to pass more quickly, but to his amazement the pick-up kept level with him.

Alarm bells sounded in his head. What was this? Was someone onto him? He removed one hand from the steering wheel and grabbed the handgun that was on the seat next to him. Clutching the weapon, he peered through the side window at the pick-up that was steadily driving alongside.

He was too high up to see into the cab, but as he glanced down he saw an astonishing thing.

A man was leaning out of the driver's side of the pick-up and peering above the roof. How on earth he was keeping the vehicle straight was anyone's guess – with difficulty, by the look of it. It was swerving dangerously. The mercenary's first reaction was to pull back again, but then he squinted. He recognized that face. He had seen him only recently after all.

Something was wrong. He didn't know what, but something was wrong. He brought the truck to a halt and watched as the pick-up stopped alongside him.

All his senses were in a heightened state of alert. This was unexpected. A surprise. And if there was one thing the mercenary didn't like, it was surprises. He clutched the handgun even more firmly, then opened the door and stepped outside into the wind and the rain. The bag containing the detonator remained safely on the passenger seat and for the moment he kept the weapon concealed inside his jacket. No point in displaying it too openly: if he needed to use the gun, much better that he had the element of surprise.

Carefully he walked round to the front of the pick-up. The man calling himself Danny did the same.

'We've got a problem,' Danny shouted above the wind.

'What do you mean?' growled the mercenary. He couldn't see what could have possibly gone wrong. His eyes darted from side to side. He was keeping a look-out, even though he didn't know what for.

Danny opened his mouth to speak. 'It's—' he started to say. But he never finished his sentence, because at that very moment he hurled himself at the other man. The mercenary crumpled to the floor as he felt the sudden weight of the man's body against his, and he grunted in pain as the small of his back slammed against the hard road. In a flash he felt Danny's hands around his throat, squeezing tightly. The mercenary gasped for breath, but no breath came.

'Where is it?' Danny demanded. His fingers dug deeply into the soft flesh of his neck.

'What?'

'The detonator,' screamed Danny. 'Where is it?'

It was nearly impossible for the mercenary to breathe, let alone speak. But he managed to get one word out.

'Why?'

'Never mind why,' Danny shouted. 'Just give it to me.'

The mercenary looked into Danny's eyes, then narrowed his own. He wanted to stop the explosion, that much was clear. But too much trouble had been gone to for him to allow that to happen. Far too much. And if the refinery didn't blow now, then that would be the end of the money coming his way. Money he wanted.

The mercenary didn't speak. He just manoeuvred his hand so that the gun was pointing upwards. The bullet would go through his jacket and straight into his attacker's belly.

And then he could get on with his work.

He was quite expressionless as he pulled the trigger. The same could not be said for Danny. The dark-haired man's eyes widened suddenly, and his grip loosened immediately. It only took a gentle nudge from the mercenary to push his attacker off him, and he watched without emotion as Danny rolled powerlessly to one side.

The mercenary pulled the gun out from his jacket. His outer garment was shredded by the force of the bullet and wet from the sudden burst of Danny's blood. With a look of distaste he quickly pulled the green jacket off and cast it onto the floor. Then, without a second look at the assailant he had just shot so calmly, he hurried back to his truck, started the ignition and drove away.

* * *

The sound of the gunshot went through Ben as surely as if the bullet itself had entered his body.

He froze; at the same time he heard Angelo gasp.

'Stay still,' he hissed. 'We don't know what's happening out there. We can't risk being seen.'

They remained as still as stones, pressed against the uncomfortable wet metal of the pick-up with the rain sheeting down on top of them. Ben strained his ears to listen to what was happening, but it was almost impossible to hear anything above the howling of the wind.

It felt like they had to wait for ever, their hearts in their throats.

And then they heard it. The low rumble of the truck moving off again.

A deathly chill seemed to freeze Ben's limbs. Only one person could be driving that truck, and that person wasn't . . .

'*Danny!*' Ben whispered. Angelo looked at him in shock and it was clear that the same thing was going through both their heads. They pushed themselves up from their crouching position and jumped over the side of the pick-up. The mercenary's truck was already disappearing into the distance. Ben looked around, desperately hoping to be able to see Danny standing, fit and well.

But that was a hope too far.

It was Angelo who saw him first. The Italian cursed under his breath in his native language as he tugged on Ben's sleeve and pointed to the ground in front of the pick-up.

Danny's body was lit up by the headlamps of the pick-up. He was lying with his face to the sky, clutching his belly, as the rain poured down on his now-pale face. He was shaking violently and Ben could see something dark seeping through his clasped hands.

Ben ran to his side and knelt down. With obvious difficulty, Danny turned to look at him. He tried to speak, but all that came out was a coarse coughing sound. A thin trickle of blood oozed from the corner of his mouth; the rain smeared it at first, then washed it clean away. Ben looked over his shoulder at Angelo.

'Help me!' he shouted. 'We need to get him into the truck.'

Angelo ran to his side; but as he did so, Danny finally managed to speak.

'Ben,' he croaked, 'you have to leave me here.'

Ben felt hot tears of anger rising in his eyes. 'I'm not leaving you anywhere,' he said from behind gritted teeth.

'He's getting away, Ben.' There was another bout of feeble coughing. 'You won't catch him if you don't leave now.'

Ben looked furiously down the road. The lights of

the mercenary's truck had completely disappeared.

'He's right, Ben,' Angelo whispered. 'We don't have any time.'

Still Ben hesitated. He had forgotten all the bad things Danny had done that day: at that moment he was just a wounded human being who needed their help.

Danny spoke again. 'Listen to me,' he hissed weakly. 'I woke up this morning expecting to die. If it happens, it's no more than I deserve. I was wrong – I understand that now. But you have to help me undo everything that's been put in motion. You *have* to stop him, both of you. For me. And for my sister.'

Danny stared at them. Somehow his pale face managed to look urgent.

And then, slowly, as if in a dream, Ben stood up. It was clear what he had to do.

'I'm coming back for you,' he told Danny hoarsely. 'Stay here, because I *am* coming back for you.'

Danny didn't reply. He didn't even look as if he had heard. His body started shaking more violently and the coughing came back. It was a pitiful sight.

Ben felt another tug on his sleeve.

'We have to hurry, Ben,' Angelo urged him. 'He's getting away.' The Italian's voice had a high-pitched note of panic in it.

Ben allowed himself one more look down at Danny

before nodding his head, reluctantly but decisively.

'All right,' he said quietly. 'Let's go.'

An absolute determination surged through him as he headed round to the driver's side of the pick-up truck.

This had to stop, he told himself. It had to stop now.

Chapter Nineteen

Danny lay on the ground. The pain in his stomach, which had been acute at first, had become numb. In fact, his whole body was numb.

It was strange. For the first time since the storm had started he found he could not hear the wind. He couldn't hear anything, actually: just the unsteady beating of his heart, and even that was getting weaker. He coughed. Something warm entered his mouth and spilled out of the sides. He supposed it should worry him, but it didn't. He was past worry now.

Danny closed his eyes. It was a peculiar thing, but he found he could almost imagine he was back home. Somewhere in the corner of his mind he heard the voices of his mother and father, as if they were in a different part of the house while he was on the brink of sleep. He couldn't quite hear what they were saying, but they sounded happy. Danny smiled weakly. That was good. It meant Basheera had returned to them.

In Danny's feeble, dreamlike state, he did not realize that this was impossible.

For a brief moment, he heard the wind again: a high-pitched wail. Or *was* it the wind? His eyes flickered open. For the second time that day he thought he heard his sister's voice in the air. He couldn't work out what it was saying; indeed it didn't really sound like it was saying *anything*. It was howling, furiously, impatiently.

And then it all came back to him.

Ben. Angelo. The detonator. He allowed his head to roll in the direction in which the pick-up truck had moved off and it was at that precise moment that the pain in his stomach returned with a vengeance. He gasped.

The howling of the wind grew angrier. Danny felt he had to do something. He tried to push himself up, but his body couldn't do what his mind had instructed and he simply fell back down uselessly onto the hard road.

His eyes started to grow dim as the shrieking overhead became more intense.

He coughed again, and then he spoke. His voice was weak, barely audible. Even if there had been anyone by his side, they would have struggled to hear him.

'I'm sorry, Basheera,' he whispered in his native language. 'I'm so, so sorry.'

And then his eyes closed again. He lay there for a few agonizing seconds before exhaling a long, rattling breath.

Danny could hear nothing any more. Nor could he feel a thing. He would not be able to whisper his sister's name ever again, and he would be able to do nothing to help Ben and Angelo in this, their final, desperate mission.

As the wind howled furiously over Danny's body, his dark hair blew around slightly. But that was the only part of him that moved.

Danny's limbs were already growing cold now. He was quite dead.

'We need to keep the headlamps off,' Ben had shouted to Angelo as he started the engine of the pick-up. Leaving Danny alone at the side of the road was the most difficult thing he'd done all day and that, he realized, was saying something. It was almost a reflex action that made him concentrate on the job in hand to keep his mind from more distressing matters. 'If he sees us approaching, he'll detonate.'

Angelo moved Danny's shotgun a bit further along the seat, then slammed his door shut. 'Er, Ben,' he said dubiously, 'won't that make it a bit difficult to drive? It's very dark out there, you know.'

Ben shrugged, determination in his face. 'We haven't got a choice,' he replied.

'Maybe he'll just think it's a different truck.'

Ben turned to look at him. 'Is that a risk you want to take?' Angelo thought about it for a few seconds, then shook his head silently. 'I didn't think so,' Ben murmured. He started the truck and moved forward, taking care to circle around Danny as he proceeded.

Every instinct Ben possessed shrieked at him to go slowly but that wasn't a luxury he had. The mercenary would be going as fast as he dared now; Ben had to go faster if he was ever going to catch up. He held his breath, gripped the steering wheel firmly and put his foot down.

It was like being on a roller coaster in the dark. The road itself was straight, but Ben still had to strain his eyes to keep a watch out for any twist in its path. Come off the road now, he knew, and it would all be over. Just keeping the truck straight, however, was a job in itself. He was used to it being buffeted by the winds, but now there was a new urgency – and a new difficulty – to what they had to do. Each time the pick-up veered from its course, he felt a sickness in his stomach as he desperately tried to hold the vehicle straight.

Ben could feel waves of nervousness coming from Angelo. His Italian friend didn't say anything, but he didn't need to. He clutched onto the passenger door with both hands. Ben couldn't see them, but he imagined that Angelo's knuckles were as white as his face. Every time the wind blew them off course and the Italian's body jolted, he would gasp. But still he kept quiet. They both knew Ben was doing the only thing he could. The way they were going, the pick-up could end up a jumble of steel on the highway, but that was a risk they just had to take.

With his eyes firmly fixed on the gloomy road ahead, Ben did not even try to look to either side of him. When Angelo shouted out 'Water!' therefore, it came as something of a surprise. He allowed his eyes to flicker left and right. There was very little ambient light, but he could just about make out what looked like the foam on huge waves in the distance. It looked like they were surrounded by sea.

'We must be on the Overseas Highway,' Angelo shouted.

'The what?'

'The Overseas Highway. It's a big road that goes over the ocean. It connects Florida to the Keys.'

Ben snapped his eyes back to the road ahead. 'How long is it?'

A brief pause. 'I don't know, Ben. I've never been on it before. Just keep the truck straight, won't you?'

As if to underline what Angelo had just said, there was a sudden gust that made Ben veer suddenly and dangerously to the left. He struggled to keep control of the pick-up.

'I'll do my best,' he shouted breathlessly at Angelo once he was straight again.

Ben was almost glad it was so dark. He didn't much like the idea of being on the Overseas Highway in the middle of a hurricane; he didn't even want to think about what would happen if the tornado caught up with them. A phrase Danny had used in the pick-up popped into his head: out of sight, out of mind. Well, the roaring waves of the ocean on either side of them weren't exactly out of mind, but as long as they were out of sight Ben could pretend he wasn't running a fool's errand. He could keep his attention focused on driving straight and looking out for the mercenary's truck ahead.

It was a few minutes later that they saw it. Hazy and indistinct in the distance, the two red lights didn't seem to be moving very fast, but Ben knew they probably were. 'That's him,' he shouted at Angelo. 'It has to be.' He didn't say out loud everything that was going through his head: *It has to be, because nobody else would be stupid enough to be out here in this.*

'How are we going to stop him?' Angelo asked. 'We can't stay hidden for long – as soon as we get a few metres away, he'll know we're on to him.'

It was a good question. Different scenarios passed through Ben's mind. He could try and get alongside the other truck and nudge the mercenary off the road. But the pick-up was the smaller of the two vehicles: in a collision it would come off worse. He could try and overtake, then bring the pick-up to a halt at right angles across the lanes; but the road was too wide for him to block it entirely, and the mercenary would simply be able to drive around them.

It was then that an idea came to him.

'Hey, Angelo,' he shouted. 'Ever fired a shotgun before?'

Angelo hesitated. 'A few times,' he said. He struggled for a moment as he searched for a phrase. 'Clay pigeon shooting, I think you call it.' Ben sensed him looking down nervously at the shotgun by his side. 'Look, Ben,' he said, his voice wavering a bit, 'I know we have to stop this man, but I don't think I could . . .'

'Don't worry,' Ben interrupted. His voice was hoarse and sore from shouting. 'That's not what I was going to suggest. But if I get close enough, do you think you could hit one of his tyres?'

Angelo stared at him. 'In the dark?' he asked. 'Ben, I don't think I'll even be able to *see* them.'

Ben thought about that. 'What if I switch the head-lamps on at the last minute. Reckon you'd have a chance?'

Angelo looked down at the shotgun. 'I don't know,' he said dubiously. 'It only holds two rounds. That means I'll only get two shots at it, and once we've let him know we're here . . .'

'He's going to find out sooner or later,' Ben interrupted. 'We might as well grab the element of surprise.'

There was a nervous silence. Suddenly the windscreen of the car was splashed with water. What scant vision Ben had disappeared for a moment.

'What was that?' he screamed.

'Rain?' Angelo suggested.

'I don't think so,' Ben shouted back. 'It's been raining all the time. That was something else.' He glanced out of the side window. 'I think it was spray from the sea. It must be getting rougher out there.' An image of the tornado they had seen flashed across Ben's brain. The thought of it made him shudder, and he tried not to think of it any more than he had to.

Angelo was gingerly picking up the shotgun. 'I'll need to open my window,' he told Ben.

'OK. Wait till I get closer.' He fixed his eyes on the lights of the truck up ahead and concentrated on narrowing the gap.

It wasn't easy. More than once his vision was blinded by spray from the sea; the road was slippery too, and it became more and more difficult to regain control of the pick-up whenever the wind knocked it off course. They drove in silence, each of them knowing that when they came within firing distance of the mercenary's truck, they wouldn't have much time to bring him to a halt; and as soon as they alerted him to their presence, they wouldn't get a second chance.

The atmosphere inside the pick-up truck seemed thick with tension as they drew closer. They were barely twenty metres away when Ben spoke again.

'Ready?' he asked Angelo.

The Italian boy took a deep breath then nodded his head slowly. 'Ready,' he replied. 'As ready as I'll ever be, anyway.'

Slowly, he wound down the window.

It felt as though they had suddenly let the storm into the truck. Ben was blinded by a blast of spray and he almost lost control of the pick-up as he wiped the water from his face. His lips tasted salt: clearly the water that had just splashed into the truck was not rain, but sea.

'Keep it steady!' Angelo yelled, a note of accusation in his voice.

'I'm trying!' Ben shouted back. The muscles in his arms burned as he tried to keep the truck on course. *'I'm trying!'* His ears were filled with the howling of the wind as, beside him, Angelo awkwardly manoeuvred the shotgun out of his window and then leaned out himself.

Keep it steady, Ben told himself. *Keep it steady*. Angelo was looking precarious, and it was clear that any sudden movement would risk throwing him out of the truck altogether.

Fifteen metres. The truck ahead kept a steady course: there was no indication that the mercenary had seen them approach.

'Closer!' Angelo shouted. 'You need to get closer!'

Ben set his jaw. The pick-up felt like it was wobbling over the slippery road, but he held to his course and increased his speed a little. The gap between them started to close.

'*Closer!*'

Ben's clothes were soaking wet, but he still found himself sweating with concentration. The gap shortened to ten metres.

'*NOW!*' Angelo roared.

With a sharp flick of his hand, Ben switched the pick-up's headlamps onto full beam. The back of the mercenary's truck was suddenly lit up. Its big wheels threw great lines of spray in its wake and for a moment the sudden light made Ben's eyes hurt. He kept a level course, though, and did his best to ignore the images that danced on the edge of his vision: great waves swelling up and crashing against the elevated highway that stretched improbably out into the sea. The very thought of all that water surrounding them made his stomach lurch, so he concentrated on the matter in hand.

'Shoot!' he yelled at Angelo. 'Now!'

There was a bang as Angelo fired a round from the shotgun. The bullet might even have found its mark if a huge wave hadn't crashed over the edge at that very moment and slammed into the side of the pick-up. Ben heard Angelo shout in pain as he was knocked harshly against the metal of the truck and suddenly the inside of the vehicle was filled with a gush of water. He skidded wildly; the truck ahead did the same. With a mammoth effort he managed to regain control of the pick-up but he knew, beyond doubt, that the mercenary would have clocked them.

Any second now he could reach for the detonator.

Any second now and all this could be for nothing.

They only had one more chance. And they had to grab it quickly.

Both vehicles had straightened up now. Angelo was still leaning out of the passenger window. Ben couldn't see his face, but he could tell the Italian boy was bracing his body, getting ready to shoot.

'Don't miss,' he whispered to himself. 'Just don't miss.'

Crack! The gun fired.

Everything seemed to happen in slow motion. Up ahead, Ben saw one of the rear wheels of the mercenary's truck explode in a blistering cloud of shredded rubber. The whole vehicle started to wobble dangerously and Ben slammed on his brakes to avoid a collision. Angelo slumped heavily back into his seat, no longer carrying the shotgun, as the pick-up turned ninety degrees and started sliding sideways along the slippery road. They were out of control, and both Ben and Angelo started shouting in fear.

But if the two of them thought *they* were in trouble, it was nothing compared to what the vehicle ahead was encountering.

At first it looked like the mercenary's truck was going to veer straight towards the edge of the raised highway. As it hurtled towards the sea, however, it seemed to flip and spin in the air. It was flying away from them, but the sight of all that metal out of control made Ben automatically fling his hands over his face in a gesture of self-protection. When he dared look again, he saw that the truck had upended itself on its roof and was scraping noisily along the road, throwing up a shower of sparks as it did so. It crashed into the barrier at the edge of the highway, destroying it completely before coming to a sudden – but deeply precarious – halt.

Both vehicles were suddenly still. Deadly still. It felt as if time itself had stopped. Even above the noise of the storm outside, Ben could hear his heart pumping and his breath came in short relieved bursts. His body was demanding a rest, but there was no time for that. The detonator was still in the possession of the mercenary, so Ben opened his door.

'Come on!' he shouted at Angelo.

He didn't wait for his Italian friend to reply before he jumped out into the road.

Chapter Twenty

The minute his feet hit the ground, Ben could sense the immense, billowing waves on either side; and as he ran to the overturned truck, he found himself choking on the thick, salty spray that had filled the air.

The mercenary's truck was lucky not to have fallen into the sea below. The vehicle's cab was dangerously close to the edge and the back wheels, which were positioned a little behind the cab, were actually overhanging. It wouldn't take much, Ben realized, for the truck to go over. He had no idea if contact with the water would activate the detonator, but that was a risk he wasn't prepared to take. Even though he felt scared to approach the edge too closely, he ran towards the upturned truck, vaguely aware that Angelo was following him.

The windscreen, which was facing into the centre of

the road, had shattered; so had the passenger windows, and the door that he approached was dented and crumpled. When Ben crouched down to look into the upside-down vehicle he saw the mercenary. The man was a mess. His face was pierced with the broken glass, and blood oozed out of each one of those many wounds. He was still strapped into the seat, but his body had slumped so that his head was pressed up against the roof of the truck.

But most alarmingly of all, he was still conscious.

To one side of him, lying on the upturned roof of the truck, there was a black bag – a rucksack. The mercenary didn't even seem to have noticed Ben: he was focusing all his attention on retrieving that bag, which was just out of reach.

The detonator, Ben thought to himself. *It's in there – it has to be!*

He moved on pure instinct. Grabbing the handle to the door, he pulled it open with a mighty tug. Only then did the mercenary appear to become aware of Ben's arrival. He turned his head and looked at him with an expression of pure hatred that was all the more sinister for the fact that he was upside down. No words were spoken, but a kind of spiteful hiss came from the mercenary's lips before he turned his attention back to the rucksack. He seemed to stretch for it with all his might.

Ben plunged his arm into the cab of the truck, past the mercenary's head and towards the rucksack. He wasn't trying to grab it so much as push it out of the man's reach.

In the end, however, he managed neither.

At first he couldn't work out what the mercenary was doing, or why. He had grabbed Ben's arm and seemed to be sizing it up, as if feeling for something. And then he jerked his arms sharply.

It was only when Ben felt his bones snap that he finally understood what was happening.

The pain was indescribable. Ben let out a shriek of agony as he lost all control of the limb, and he offered no resistance at all as the mercenary pushed him out of the way. He fell heavily to the ground, then watched helplessly as the mercenary's fingers clasped the fabric of the bag. There was a look of triumph on the man's face: he plunged his hand into the bag and started to pull something out.

'*NO!*' Ben roared. He tried to push himself up, but the devastating pain in his broken arm stopped him from doing anything. '*Don't do it!*' he yelled. '*Just don't do it!*'

But the mercenary ignored him. He had it in his hands now, a small metal object no bigger than a mobile phone.

That was it. Ben stared in frozen horror, realizing

there was nothing more he could do to stop what was going to happen.

He'd played his last card.

He had lost.

He opened his mouth to shout again, but the sound never left his throat, because just then he saw Angelo.

The Italian boy appeared on the other side of the truck. The mercenary hadn't clocked him – he was too busy clutching the detonator, gazing at it with a look of greedy elation as he prepared to activate it. But from his position on the wet ground Ben watched, heart in mouth, as his friend ripped the other door open and dived into the cab of the truck.

The mercenary was completely taken by surprise. He roared in anger and started to struggle, but it wasn't enough. Angelo's fingers curled round the detonator. He snapped it away and then wriggled back outside.

The man squirmed as he tried to release himself from the truck's seatbelt while Angelo sprinted round the front of the vehicle to Ben. '*L'ho preso!*' he yelled. 'I've got it! I've got—'

He stopped and took one look at Ben.

'What's the matter?' he asked. Clearly Ben looked as bad as he felt.

'My arm!' Ben screamed over the noise of the waves and the wind. 'I think it's broken.' As he spoke, he felt himself being sprayed yet again with salty water; then he furrowed his brow. Angelo was looking out to sea and he had a strange look in his eyes.

'Ben,' he said quietly, 'move.' And then he shouted it, pulling Ben up by his good arm. '*Move, Ben! Now!*'

Ben felt himself being pulled to his feet, and as he did so he glanced out to sea. It was only then that he realized what Angelo had seen. For a split second it looked as if there was something rising out of the ocean – some huge, shapeless beast, like something out of a nightmare.

It was nothing of the sort, of course. It was the ocean itself, swelling hugely and hurling at them a titanic wave, the very size of which made Ben's eyes bulge.

Instinctively, he ran.

They managed to get as far as the pick-up. Ben threw himself to the floor and flung his good arm around one of the truck's tyres, squeezing and gripping onto it with all his might. He tucked his head down, took a deep breath, braced himself and closed his eyes. When the wave hit, he knew, it would carry with it all the force of the ocean.

He wasn't wrong.

It didn't feel like water thumping into his body. It felt like something solid. Instantly all the air was pumped out of him; on a reflex he tried to draw breath again – his lungs simply filled with water that was crashing over and around him. So it was that he had no breath in him to be able to scream, not even when the water smashed against his broken arm. The rushing in his ears was like an explosion. All he could do was hold onto that truck and hope – against all hope – that this wasn't the end.

It was with a sinking, sickening feeling that he felt the truck move. Not even that great hunk of iron could withstand the force of the angry sea – it slid towards the other side of the road and spun round so that Ben – blinded by the wave – could not tell where he was or in which direction he was pointing.

Any second now, he thought to himself, and I'll be pushed over into the sea. When that happened it wouldn't matter that he was clutching hold of the pick-up; but he gripped it a little tighter, just in case.

Then, as quickly as it had come, the wave subsided. Ben was dizzy from lack of air. He felt himself coughing up salt water, and for a long moment it didn't even register with him that he was still on the road. He let go of the truck, wiped the water from his eyes and looked around.

The truck was still the right way up, but it had moved about twenty metres back the way they had come and towards the other side of the road. Ben looked back over towards the mercenary's truck. Then he blinked.

It was no longer there.

He squinted his eyes and looked around again. There was no doubt about it. The mercenary hadn't survived the impact of the wave. He was gone.

And then he realized something else. He was alone. The mercenary might have disappeared, but so had . . .

'*Angelo!*' he screamed. '*Angelo! Where are you?*'

Ben stopped to listen for a response. There was none: just the sound of the storm and Ben's panicked breathing.

He spun around, doing his best to ignore the pain in his limp arm. His eyes were still smarting from the salt water; he squinted them as he peered into the darkness, desperately trying to see Angelo.

He couldn't. What he saw instead was something quite different.

The moon had appeared again, bright and full. And out to sea, in the distance – though not as far as the last time he had seen it – was the tornado. Ben blinked, transfixed for a few moments by that awesome, awful sight. There was no doubt about it. It was coming this way. How fast it was moving he couldn't tell, but the last place he wanted to be if that thing hit the Overseas Highway was here.

But what about Angelo? He couldn't leave until he was sure that his friend was . . .

The very thought made him shudder.

And as he shuddered, he heard a voice.

It was faint. Barely audible above all the other noise. But it was definitely a voice. Shouting. Ben made out a single word: '*Help!*' He spun round again, trying to see where it was coming from.

There was nothing.

He ran towards where they had been when the wave hit. The voice was a bit louder here, but still he saw no sign of Angelo. Apart from Ben and the pick-up truck, the road was deserted. He glanced nervously towards the tornado. If he was going to get out of here, he had to leave quickly. He had to leave now.

It was only then that he saw him.

Angelo wasn't on the road; the wave had thrown him to the edge and now he was hanging onto the raised barrier with a single hand. Ben sprinted towards him. The face of his Italian friend was etched with a mixture of concentration, exhaustion and sheer terror. One hand was taking all his weight, and with an immense struggle he raised the other over the edge of the barrier.

He was still clutching the detonator.

'I can't hold on much longer, Ben,' he shouted urgently. 'Take it! Take the detonator! We can't let it fall into the water with me.'

As he spoke, Angelo's grip faltered. Half of his face disappeared behind the barrier, leaving only his eyes in view. They were urgent and terrified as he waved the detonator in the air.

Ben knew he was right. He knew he should grab the detonator first. But somehow he simply couldn't. He fixed Angelo with a steely, determined stare, then used his good arm to clutch onto his friend's wrist – the one that was holding the barrier.

'Let go,' he hissed. 'I can't pull you back if you're still holding on.'

Angelo hesitated.

'*Let go!*' Ben insisted. It was a leap of faith, he knew that. But it was one that had to be made.

Angelo's fingers relaxed; all of a sudden, Ben was supporting all his friend's weight.

Then he pulled.

Battered and exhausted, Ben felt like he had no strength in him, but he didn't give up. One-handed, he tugged at Angelo's arm with every last bit of power he possessed, slowly dragging his friend – and the detonator – over the barrier towards him. On the fringes of his vision was the tornado, watching over them, waiting to strike; and all around them were the sounds and sights of the storm and the raging seas.

Ben ignored it all. He ignored the pain in his broken arm; he ignored the spray that was all around them. He just pulled for all he was worth.

It took nearly a minute to haul Angelo in. The Italian boy fell heavily onto the ground, but he did not let go of the detonator. He lay on his back, panting; but there was still no time to rest. The very moment Angelo was on the road, Ben's attention was elsewhere.

The tornado was coming. They *had* to get away.

'Get in the truck,' Ben bellowed. 'You'll have to drive – I can't with this broken arm.' He winced as he spoke, trying to ignore the wooziness that was creeping over his body.

Angelo struggled to his feet and together they hurried to the pick-up. 'I can't,' he replied as they ran. 'I've never driven. I don't know how.'

They were at the truck now. Ben looked nervously once more at the tornado. 'When that thing gets here,' he shouted, 'it's going to rip up everything in its path.' He turned to Angelo. 'All right,' he shouted. 'I'll drive. But you'll have to help me.'

Angelo looked unsure of himself, but he nodded and they both jumped into the pick-up.

It was saturated inside, dripping like the inside of a shower cubicle. Ben sat behind the wheel, his broken arm hanging limply by his side, then awkwardly used his other hand to turn the ignition. The engine coughed and spluttered, but it did not turn over.

Ben cursed, then tried again.

Nothing.

He looked at Angelo. 'I can't keep doing this,' he said. 'I'll flood the engine.'

'Er, Ben,' Angelo said tensely. 'We haven't really got

time to wait for this thing to dry out. Either we get it going, or we run.'

The two of them looked at the road ahead. It stretched off into the darkness: neither of them needed to say out loud that if they tried to do it on foot, they'd never make it.

Ben took a deep breath and turned the key one more time. The engine choked alarmingly but then, suddenly, it sprang into life. They exchanged a relieved glance.

'Knock it into drive,' Ben instructed.

Angelo did as he was told and Ben gingerly moved forward. His arm was shrieking in pain and his whole body was sweating, but he tried to ignore it as he accelerated, and soon they were thundering along the slippery road once again.

Ben did his best not to look in the rear-view mirror, knowing that if he caught another glimpse of the tornado it would do nothing for his concentration. He just kept his eye on the road ahead. Now and then the windscreen would be splattered with sea water and his vision obscured. But he just kept going, keeping the truck straight with his good arm, all the while doing what he could to ignore the pain in his other one.

He could never have kept it up for long. They had been driving for little more than ten minutes when he started to feel faint. His foot slipped from the accelerator; the pick-up started to slow down.

'Don't stop,' Angelo shouted, rousing Ben from his moment of faintness. 'I think I can see land. Keep going.'

Ben's foot felt for the accelerator again; he increased his speed and did everything he could to keep his concentration up. Angelo could clearly tell he was having difficulties, because he kept talking, loudly and in tones of encouragement. Ben had no idea what he was saying, however. He wasn't even listening. He was just concentrating on getting off the Overseas Highway and onto Key Largo.

When he finally saw the first of the Florida Keys, he felt like a condemned man who had been given a last-minute reprieve. A huge billboard flapped in the wind. 'WELCOME TO KEY LARGO' it read in big, bright letters; but the island didn't look very welcoming. Nowhere looked welcoming in the middle of the night in this kind of weather. Ben was vaguely aware of the wind-devastated buildings up ahead, but he paid them no attention. They were a familiar sight now, after all. The pick-up truck screamed onto dry land and Ben travelled away from the coast for a good couple of minutes before finally allowing his foot to slip from the accelerator. The truck slowed down gradually as Ben coasted along the main road that was still mercifully deserted. And finally it shuddered and stalled to halt.

Ben glanced to one side. Angelo was there, ashen-faced and soaking wet. But in his hand he still held the detonator. Safely. Soundly. Clutching it for all he was worth.

It was the last thing Ben saw before he slumped, exhausted and in agony, over the steering wheel of the vehicle, and then passed out.

Back out at sea, the tornado whirled and twisted. It sucked up huge amounts of sea water and then spat them out again, all the while making its relentless way in the direction of the Overseas Highway.

It reached that huge structure barely minutes after Ben and Angelo had evacuated it. It only took a few seconds to rip up the huge girders of concrete, steel and tar from which the road had been constructed; and only a few seconds to throw it out again, leaving a scene of utter devastation in its wake.

And had anybody been there, they might have noticed a curious thing. It was a truck that seemed to erupt from the murky, stormy waters of the sea, as though it were defying the laws of science and nature and taking flight. It was nature herself, however, who sucked it up into the sky, spun it round like a stone in a sling and then hurled it even further out to sea, where it broke up into a hundred pieces as it slammed against the water.

But nobody was there, and a good thing too. Because no human could have survived standing in the course of that immense, powerful freak of nature.

The twister continued its way out to sea, howling and roaring as it spun into the empty void of the night.

Epilogue

One week later. Miami International Airport.

Angelo had bought Ben a small cup of thick, black Italian coffee, but he didn't really feel like drinking it. Instead he sat at the edge of the airport café, watching the hubbub all around him.

There was still a sense of repressed panic. Nothing like the aftermath of Hurricane Jasmine, of course. But a sense of panic nevertheless. Florida would take months to recuperate from the effects of the storms, if not years, and they were still in the middle of the hurricane season. Nobody really expected another battering of that magnitude, but still – Ben had the impression that there were some nervous flyers in the airport that day. And he was one of them.

He winced slightly and looked down at his arm. It

was encased in plaster from the wrist up to the shoulder. It ached dully, but that wasn't the worst thing: the itchiness of the skin was driving him to distraction. There was no way he could scratch it, though, so he tried to divert his attention by sipping on the coffee. It was incredibly bitter and he pulled a sour face. He liked his Italian friend a lot – after everything they had been through together, they were almost brothers – but the guy had a rotten taste in drinks.

Just then, Angelo reappeared. He was clutching a newspaper as he battled his way through the crowds and he nodded at Ben as he approached and sat down. He pointed at the coffee.

'Not drinking that?'

'Er, no,' Ben replied. 'Delicious and everything, but I just don't fancy it.'

Angelo shrugged, laid the newspaper on the table and downed the coffee in one. Ben glanced at the front page of the paper. The picture it bore was predictable enough. Every newspaper had shown a similar image each day for the past week: the Overseas Highway, battered and destroyed, and the huge gap in the road that had been ripped out by the storms. No one knew how long it would take to repair the road, and everybody was astonished that nobody was reported killed as a result of the disaster – though Ben and Angelo knew better, of course.

The death toll elsewhere, however, had been a different matter. At the latest count 300 people had lost their lives in the storms. An awful statistic, and already people were looking for someone to blame – as if anyone could be blamed for such a freak of nature. Ben couldn't help wondering, though, what the reaction would be if things had gone just a little differently and the South Miami Oil Refinery had turned into a fireball. Even now the thought made him shudder.

It had been an exhausting week. Ben had woken in an ambulance with Angelo by his side. They'd given him morphine for the pain, then plastered his arm in a makeshift hospital that had been set up in a large community centre. They'd stayed there till morning, by which time the storm had abated. Ben and Angelo were then immediately airlifted from Key Largo to the mainland in a military Chinook.

It had seemed odd that they were airlifted before anyone else, but when they saw the three grim-faced FBI officers waiting for them as their helicopter touched down in Miami, it all started making a bit more sense. The FBI men had told him curtly he needed a responsible adult present; Ben had immediately thought of Alec. The old man was walked into the room in which Ben was being held only hours later. He looked tired and stooped; Ben learned that his house had been torn away, but at least he hadn't been hurt.

The expression of relief on his face when he saw Ben safe and sound was noticeable.

'I thought you were going to try and stay out of trouble, matey,' he had said as he took Ben's hand, shaken it warmly, then ignored his natural diffidence and given him a hug.

'Yeah,' Ben had replied. 'Well I did try.'

The interrogation took two days. They wanted to know everything: the hijacking, Danny, the mercenary. Ben had wearily told them the whole story, and when he had finished they had made him start all over again. They separated him from Angelo, called him 'kid' and eyed him with mistrust. Even Alec looked as if he thought Ben was embellishing the truth, though loyal to the last he said nothing.

But then reports started to come in: reports that substantiated his story, especially from members of the crew and passengers on their doomed flight, all of whom seemed also to have made it. As that happened, the looks of mistrust started to be replaced with stares of astonishment and respect. Ben supposed it should make him feel good, but it didn't. He just felt awkward, and he wanted to go home.

Angelo too was given the all-clear, as well as several wide-eyed stares of disbelief when the FBI guys realized what he'd been through – and what he had achieved.

Eventually, they had given permission for Ben to

leave the country. In less than an hour now, he would be boarding a flight to London where his parents would be meeting him. He couldn't wait.

'Hey,' Angelo said. 'I want to show you something.' He put down the coffee cup and opened the paper.

'You know what?' Ben said. 'I think I've read quite enough about the storms.' But Angelo shook his head, a mysterious smile on his face, and pointed to something else. The article he showed Ben was hidden away on the financial pages towards the back, after all the many pictures and reports of the storm damage. Ben read it curiously.

The Bandini Oil Corporation has recently announced a review of its operations in the Indian Ocean. Fabio Bandini, CEO of the corporation, said the review was due to internal restructuring and a realignment of the country's ethical policies. The share price dropped twenty points on the news.

Ben raised an eyebrow. 'Fabio Bandini?' he asked.
Angelo nodded. 'My dad.'
'You persuaded him?'
Angelo closed the newspaper. 'I made a promise to Danny, didn't I?'

At the name of Danny, they both fell silent. His death hadn't been reported – he was just one of the many who had lost their lives in the storms – and Ben wasn't quite sure how he felt about it. The guy had tried to kill them, after all. But it wasn't quite as simple as that. Danny had been brave at the end – a courageous man who had done the wrong things for the right reasons. And in the end he had seen the light and made good his mistakes. Ben's view of the world had got a little bit more complicated in the last week, and he wasn't sure how he felt about that.

Angelo broke the silence. 'Come on,' he said, looking up at the nearby information board. 'They're calling your flight.'

Ben nodded silently, then stood up as Angelo took his hand luggage for him.

'You'll come to Italy sometime to see me?' Angelo asked. He grinned slightly. 'The weather's normally pretty good.'

Ben smiled. 'No storms?' he asked.

'Well, now and then. But the sun always comes out again afterwards.'

'Sounds good to me,' said Ben. 'I could do with a bit of sunshine.'

Angelo nodded enthusiastically. '*Anch'io*,' he replied. 'Me too.' And with that they started walking, unobserved by the other passengers – none of whom knew what they had been through – into the airport crowds and towards the aeroplane that would fly Ben across the Atlantic, and back home.

Author's note

The Florida Keys were originally connected to the US mainland by the Overseas Railroad. This was partially destroyed by a hurricane in 1935 and was replaced by the Overseas Highway.

The Atlantic hurricane season lasts from June to November. The duration and strength of hurricanes has increased by 50 per cent over the past three decades. Scientists do not know for sure whether this is a result of global warming, but they *do* know that heat is a key factor in the formation of hurricanes. It seems likely, therefore, that as the temperature of the oceans and the atmosphere continues to rise, hurricanes are going to get worse.